Tales from the Dark Woods

Tales from the Dark Woods

Brendan DuBois

Five Star • Waterville, Maine

Five Star First Edition Mystery Series.
First Printing.

Published in 2002 in conjunction with Tekno Books and
Ed Gorman.

Set in 11 pt. Plantin by Liana M. Walker.

Printed in the United States on permanent paper.

Library of Congress Cataloging-in-Publication Data

DuBois, Brendan.
    Tales from the dark woods / Brendan DuBois.
      p. cm.—(Five Star first edition mystery series)
    Contents: Dark corridor—Final marks, final secrets—
Not much of a trade—The necessary brother—Thieves—
The dark snow—Rapunzel's revenge—Customer's
choice—The star thief—The men on the wall.
    ISBN 0-7862-4846-7 (hc : alk. paper)
    1. Detective and mystery stories, American. I. Title.
    II. Series.
  PS3554.U2564 T3 2002
  813′.54—dc21   2002029943

This collection is dedicated with thanks and affection
to the memory of Cathleen Sullivan,
my editor at *Alfred Hitchcock's Mystery Magazine*.

Table of Contents

Foreword

Welcome to this collection of some of my favorite short stories, written over quite a number of years, covering quite a number of themes. Instead of going into great detail here of how each of these stories came about, let me start by discussing the title.

The title suggests that all of these pieces of short fiction have a basis in the rural countryside, such as the small towns in New Hampshire that I know and love. While this is true in most of these stories, not all of them take place in such a bucolic setting. One takes place in Quebec City. Another takes place in an urban nightmare, where chaos and anarchy have returned and the police have retreated. And yet another—for the most part—takes place in sunny Florida.

But what all of these stories may have in common is something inside of me that recalls growing up in quiet New Hampshire, where empty and ill-paved country roads let into dark valleys and remote landscapes. Where mountain ranges at night are lit only by moon and starlight. And where odd sounds and screeches come from the woods at night, sounds of hunting and death and mystery. As a child in such a place, the dark woods were a constant mystery, and a constant source of tales, passed on, from one family to the next, from one generation to another. There were stories told around campfires, on porch fronts during rainy days, and at night, in bedrooms, under the covers and with flashlights grasped in small hands. Stories about ghosts and witches and Indians, stories that arose from where we lived and worked and played.

Even centuries later, there was something about our surroundings in peaceful New Hampshire that spoke of a violent and mysterious past. I had—and still have—a fascination with the early history of my home state.

Even as a boy, I knew the names of the Indian tribes in the area, the Algonquins and Micmacs and Abenakis. I knew of the bloody history when the first settlers arrived in the early 1600's, and how massacres were matched by retaliations from the other side. I also learned the old stories as well, of witchcraft and lights in the skies, of sea monsters off the Atlantic Coast, and newer stories, as well, of German U-boats stalking shipping off our coastline, and the ever-present Soviet menace, kept at bay by nuclear-armed bombers from a nearby Strategic Air Command airbase.

All these tales, all these stories, percolated in my consciousness and mind as I grew into an adult. And when it became time for me to start writing short fiction, it made sense to first go to the very place where stories had meaning for me, in the tales told to each other by children, or told to us by the fabled tribe known as grown-ups.

Much of my short fiction does take place in rural New Hampshire, Vermont, or Maine. But others don't. Yet I think there is some connection, some thread that runs through all of these tales. It's the thought about the shadows, the dark places that inhabit all of us, that inhabit our fears and our hopes. It's the dark places that resonate with me, and I hope, with some of you as well, for it's the dark places where, I believe, the best of mystery fiction takes place.

So welcome here, to my own place and home in the dark woods, where the tales of mystery and suspense still rule.

Enjoy your visit, and enjoy these stories as well.

Brendan DuBois
Exeter, New Hampshire
May 2002

They say you never forget your first, and that's certainly the case with my first published short story, "Dark Corridor." Previously I had written scores and scores of science fiction and fantasy short stories. All had been rejected, including this one. However, I decided it had a bit of mystery to it, so I sent it off to "Ellery Queen's Mystery Magazine." A few weeks later, I got a contract back in the mail, and not a rejection slip. That's when I decided I wanted to be a mystery author, instead of a science fiction author.

Dark Corridor

It was getting on toward dark when he decided it was time to go out and try again. He had spent three days so far at this beach resort in a motel room, coming back unsuccessful early each morning, falling asleep on the bed after taking only his boots off. He had relaxed that afternoon, knowing he wouldn't go out and work again until the sun had set, and he had swum thirty laps in the motel pool, keeping to himself and ignoring the bikini-clad women reclining about him, steaming in their suntan oil. The one he was looking for wasn't at the pool, and he was sure he would find her tonight and finish the job.

He came out of the small bathroom, wiping the flecks of shaving cream from his chin. It was a clean room, as rooms go, and in the past two years he had stayed in so many they seemed to blend together in his mind. This one had a double bed, color television, a small writing desk, and a bureau with a mirror. His suitcase was under the bed and only his coat was hanging in the closet. A large window looked over the beach—Tyler Beach, it was called—and the white sands that stretched to the Atlantic.

He was in New Hampshire. He wasn't sure if he had ever been in New Hampshire before. The map with the little red dots that charted the places he had been in the past two years was stashed in the trunk of his car. That would tell him, but it wasn't important now. It was time to get dressed. In the little buzzing and quivering in the back of his mind, he could feel it all right—he would get it done tonight.

After pulling on his worn jeans, black T-shirt, and leather jacket, he slipped on his boots and looked at himself in the mirror, combing his shower-wet black hair and trying to hide most of the furrowed pink scar that angled down from his forehead to his ear. He frowned at his image in the mirror, smiled, and then touched the scar once almost tenderly.

Two years. He had once worked at a newspaper, sitting at a computer terminal, editing copy and dummying pages. Then came the day at work when a piece of scaffolding collapsed and cracked his skull with a sound like a pistol shot.

The next few months had been odd, waking up and sleeping, fading in and out, and after his discharge he had tried to go back to the newspaper. But there were the headaches, the damn headaches, and the bright lights and images that came whenever he closed his eyes, and in another month he was gone from the paper, receiving a disability check every week. There had been some brain damage, but the doctors were never quite sure how much or what kind. It was hard to remember what they had said. It was even hard to remember what newspaper he had worked at or what city he had come from. It was out in the Midwest somewhere, that was all he could be sure of. That, and the memory of the images and impulses that came to him during the time at the hospital.

He knelt down and dragged his suitcase from underneath

the bed—it had a combination lock, and when he opened it he removed his tools for the night's work. The 9mm pistol went into an ankle holster and the folded stiletto went snug into his jeans. The wire garrote, with its two thumb loops, went into his jacket. He flexed his hands after standing up, took a deep breath, and went out the door, locking it behind him . . .

Outside, the night air was clear and cool, with a salty tang from the ocean. He walked up the main boulevard, a long row of open shops, bars, motels, video arcades, and fast-food restaurants. Lights flickered and there was the screaming jangling of the video games and the smell of pizza, fried dough, and popcorn. The cement sidewalk was crowded with tourists and beachgoers, and on his right two lanes of one-way traffic inched north. Streetlights and neon signs kept everything bright. He walked along, eyes and ears open, letting everything sink into him. He felt the quivering inside of him again and his palms were moist. A good sign. He would be lucky tonight.

He stopped at a newsstand for a paper and sat on a nearby park bench. He flipped through the pages, not only reading the stories but checking how the editors and paste-up people had laid out the stories and chosen the headlines. It was one of the few links he had to the time before the accident. All that happened after the accident had remained with him, but everything before then was murky and dark. It was like trying to remember the day-to-day events of an August month when you were only five years old.

Newspapers were the one thing he liked to read. He liked comparing the ones he picked up in his travels, from the big dailies to the small weeklies that ran feed-store ads on the front page. The stories were always interesting.

Sometimes, and only a few times at that, he had seen stories of his work appear on a front page, or at least on page two or three. Seeing the stories upset him in a small way. He was proud of his work now, but it was a private thing, not something to be shared and used to titillate others. He had also seen many stories of other people out there engaged in similar work, and he had clipped and saved those stories as research. The stories were different, but the subject matter was always the same.

He looked up from the paper as he flipped the pages to the sports section. Tourists of all types flowed past him—large Canadian families speaking in French, groups of teenaged girls trying to look twenty and women of thirty or older trying to look twenty. The boys and young men were loud, dressed almost in uniform—jeans, sneakers, and T-shirts—and several carried large cassette radios. They were all ignorant of how easy it was. With a car and some luck and a good knife, you could do his type of work one day in New York City, say, and the next day, when the cops were trying to piece together clues and line up witnesses, you could be in Pennsylvania. The day after that, while the cops were trying to figure out motives, you could be in Maryland, getting ready for another job.

And they were doing it. The dark was full of it. Driving along the side roads late at night, looking for a classical station on the radio, he would feel them out there, doing their work—in Seattle, Los Angeles, Atlanta, New Orleans. He could see them, sometimes almost smell them.

He got up, dropping the folded newspaper on the bench. There was time to waste and he strolled around the strip of shops, letting his mind and the electric impulses move him along. He was getting closer. He went inside a T-shirt store and browsed through the different-colored shirts. The shop was little more than a large room, with the shirts hanging off suspended racks. Rock music boomed from speakers mounted on the walls. The fabric of one of the shirts slipped softly through his fingers as he looked at the woman clerk. She was in her early twenties, with a dark tan and short brown hair. She came from behind the counter to help a fat tourist standing at a rack with his cameras and shopping bags. Her denim miniskirt was molded against her hips and she wore black seamed stockings and high heels. A light-blue T-shirt with a seagull on it was tucked taut and snug into her waist. He listened to her laugh and watched her right leg bounce in time with the music. He stared at her. Was she the one? He closed his eyes and then looked at her again. No. She wasn't.

Outside again, he felt the urge to keep moving. He trusted his urges. Since the accident, they had never been wrong. For a few weeks after he left the newspaper, he had stayed at home, trying to ignore the new feelings and impulses and images that urged him to roam at night. But it was like trying to lie in bed and ignore a fire underneath it.

That first night, he had wandered along aimlessly, the handgun heavy in his coat pocket, until he went down a dark street and saw the flickering movement of a person coming toward him. He had taken the gun out instinctively and pulled the trigger one-two-three-four-five-six, not stopping even when the shadow had screamed and crumpled to the slick asphalt. He had run home and not gone out for a week, not until he had seen the newspaper story that told him who the shadow had been. Then he knew he would do it again.

He paused for a moment among the crowd, noticing a green-and-white police cruiser crawling along next to the sidewalk. Two cops in the front seat scanned the crowd and he knew better than to walk quickly away or to run. He stood still, watching them go by, praying they wouldn't stop and find an excuse to search him. They would find his weapons, and they would start checking the computer records. And if they found the map, it would be a simple thing to start matching up the red dots with his work. He would certainly go to jail and might even die. He was not about to let that happen. His work was too important.

Inside an open restaurant, he sat on a swivel stool and ordered a pepperoni pizza slice and a Coke. It was when he was munching on the pizza that he spotted the waitress on the other side of the restaurant and knew he had found her. She was blonde and wore her long hair in a French braid. Even though she was wearing a blue-and-white waitress uniform, she stood out. She had a nice figure, but it was her smile that attracted him, the way her eyes shone at the customers, full of life. He saw her glance up at the clock and he knew she would be leaving soon. He smiled in anticipation. The waiting was over. Soon he would be done with this job and he could move on.

Early on during his work, he remembered as he finished his pizza, he had actually had a few regrets, but the time in— was it Indianapolis?—had changed him. Standing in the woman's bedroom, over her still and bloody-sheet-covered form, he had stared in amazement at the photos she had on her wall, displayed like trophies, photos that screamed at him, and since then he had no regrets. He swallowed the last of the Coke. The images and the flashes were coming on stronger. It was like watching a movie preview in a smoky, ill-lit theater. He never saw all of what was going to happen, but he saw enough.

He walked back out to the boardwalk and wandered, listening to the traffic, the people, and the boom of the ocean striking the sand. Then it was time.

He went back to the restaurant and there she was, heading out along the sidewalk, her French braid bouncing with each step. She carried a purse and wore an open cloth jacket. He tailed her. There was a side street up ahead that stretched away from the beach, but she walked past it, even though he knew she would go down that street in a few more minutes. She stopped at an open-counter place that sold coffee and pastries and bought a cup of coffee in a plastic cup from a young guy she smiled at in a different way than she did her customers.

He touched the knife in his jeans. *Ah, my friend,* he thought, looking at the counter man, *if only you knew what is waiting here for your sweetheart.* She leaned forward and got a quick kiss from the counter man. By the time she turned, he had already slipped down the side street.

The street was like a dark corridor, with only a few weak streetlights. It was narrow and crowded with parked cars. There were no stores or bars, just rows of motel units, garages, and dark cottages. He walked down the middle of the road, his boot heels clicking against the tar surface. Inside, he was trembling so hard he thought his hands would shake. The flashes in his mind were like a strobe now.

He reached the end of the road and circled back, cutting through some back yards, dodging clotheslines and barbecue grills. He crept silently up a dirt driveway until he came back to the street and he crouched behind a pile of bulging garbage bags. He could hear a far off television set, but the cottages around him seemed empty. Good. No witnesses.

His eyes adjusted to the darkness and he took deep, silent breaths. He tried to ease the tension and again touched the knife in his jeans. It would come out soon enough. The garrote was for backup and he hated to use the pistol, it made so much noise. Besides, he enjoyed the knife.

He saw her approach, her heels making a sharp clicking on the asphalt. He eased the knife out. It felt good in his hand, a comfortable weight. She came closer and he shook his head in wonderment. Why did they always do this? Why did they do such stupid things, like walking alone on a dark and empty street? As she came past only a few feet from him, he saw she was sipping from the coffee container and he stood slowly up, watching her walk on.

Now there was the other shadow, moving up from the opposite side of the street and quickstepping across toward her. He took two fast steps out in the street and was behind the shadow, his forearm around the throat. He kicked the man's legs out from under him and dragged him behind some garbage bags. He knelt over him, one hand on the man's mouth, the other holding his knife, both of his knees digging hard into the man's outstretched wrists.

The waitress had stopped beside a streetlight and looked back. He felt the man convulsing beneath him, trying to get up, and he ignored him, watching the waitress, wishing her home. She shook her head and kept walking. *Good for you, sweetheart,* he thought, *be safe. Always.*

He went back to the man struggling underneath him. Even in the darkness he could tell the man wasn't clean. He smiled in anticipation as he removed his left hand from the mouth and thrust his other hand down hard toward the throat. He sat back quickly on his haunches and listened with satisfaction to the harsh gurgling that eventually faded away to a wheezing. He wiped his knife clean on the man's pants leg and returned it to his jeans, then started the search. In one pocket was a switchblade, in another a woman's nylon stocking. He left both on the man's sticky chest.

The street was clear. He walked back up it and in a few minutes he was mingling with the crowd along the boardwalk. He was happy, with a warm feeling of release. It had gone like all the rest. Some people had strange talents, he thought. Some could multiply large figures in their minds and others made millions in the stock market. He was able to thwart those who preyed on innocent people.

Back at the motel, he would check out shortly. He would make another dot on the map in the car and then start driving. This time he would head south.

I went through twelve years of a Catholic education and in addition to getting an excellent grounding in writing, science, history and other disciplines, I was also instilled with a healthy sense of guilt and fear. In this story, both guilt and fear come into play over a long-ago report card with poor marks.

Final Marks, Final Secrets

It started again, a month after I married my wife Annie. We were in our new apartment in a small North Shore town outside of Boston, and we were playing a game newlyweds probably think up all the time. It was Annie's idea and though I smiled and played along with her, it felt like a cold ice cube was being run up and down my back.

The game was called "Secrets," and we went back and forth, telling each other past secrets we had kept from our families and our friends, but not from ourselves. No, not that, at least. We were in the living room and the sliding glass door to the deck was open, and I saw fireflies dance and blink over the Bellamy River as we played. I looked away, suddenly not liking the door being so open. Strawberry daiquiris in hand and candles on an oak dining table, we talked the night away. Annie had just told me of a time when she was seventeen and had spent the night in Boston, partying, when she was supposed to be with a high school friend. And before that, I had told her about my first and only shoplifting offense, when I was twelve and stole a *Playboy* just for a chance to see what was hidden behind those glossy covers.

I took a leisurely sip from my frozen strawberry drink,

which was in a delicate and long glass, one of the countless wedding gifts from nameless aunts or uncles that cluttered our apartment. I wondered how long it would take before "Uncle Ray's table" became our table, and I wondered how long before the game was over. But in the candlelight Annie's blue eyes were laughing at me.

"C'mon, Lew, it's your turn for a secret," she said. "You know secrets aren't healthy for a modern marriage."

The flickering light made her blonde hair sparkle and looking at her I had a warm feeling that everything, at long last, was right. I had met the right woman, I had made the right choices, and things were going to be perfect. Annie was a layout artist for an advertising company in Boston, while I was a wire editor for one of the city's two largest newspapers. I had gone many miles to get here, and I hoped I was happy.

"Sorry," I said. "My life isn't that sordid. I'm squeaky clean; even your parents think so."

She stuck out her tongue. "Maybe, Lew, but your parents told me a few secrets. Especially your mother."

The ice cube was back. "My mother?"

"Right." Annie picked up her matching glass and took a long swallow, and put her drink down. A breeze from the river made the candles flicker. She gave me an arch look with her eyebrows. "Your mother. About the time you were at that Catholic high school and forged your report card."

I tried to smile but I failed. I picked up my glass and there was a sharp *crack* and my hand felt suddenly cold and then warm. Annie screamed and I looked down, and part of the shattered glass was still in my hand. The dull pink of the frozen strawberry was dripping down my wrist, joined by the shockingly bright red of something else. *Good God,* I thought. *He's come back.*

★ ★ ★ ★ ★

Lewis Callaghan was fourteen years old and was certain of one thing—by tomorrow, Saturday, he would be dead.

He slouched low in his classroom seat, trying to be as inconspicuous as possible, though it felt like a spotlight was trained on him. Like every other male in St. Mary's High School in North Manchester, he wore black shoes, black pants, a white shirt, and a blue necktie with S.M.H.S. in gold thread in the center. The windows were open for the first time that year, promising spring with a warm breeze and the smell of wet earth, but he could only concentrate on one thing—what he held in his sweaty hands.

It was a folded piece of white cardboard, with the school seal on the outside and his handwritten name and "Grade 9" underneath it. Inside were columns listing school subjects and inside the report card was his death warrant.

He sank lower in his seat.

A few hours ago he had watched Sister Juanita, sitting behind her large wooden desk in her flowing black and white habit, as she reached into a side drawer and came up with the blank report cards for that semester. She had slowly transferred the marks for each student from a leather-bound ledger on her desk to the blank cards, and once she had looked up at him and glared at Lewis with those cold blue eyes of hers. At that look his heart felt like stone. He was dead.

Lewis opened the report card just a bit, ashamed of what was in there, not wanting anyone else to see the scarlet mark. History, B +. Geography, B. English, A. Religion, A. French, B. And Algebra, F.

F.

His hands felt dirty. God, he had never gotten a D in his life, never mind an F. His parents were away visiting his aunt and uncle in Rhode Island and were due back tomorrow, and that was the day he was going to die. He was sure of it. Up on the pale green wall, over the clock that said he had ten minutes left of the school day, was a crucifix. He said a Hail Mary, remembering the miracles he had read about in religion class. Please God, just this once.

He opened the card again. It still said F.

Around him the other students—the boys dressed like him, the girls in their plaid skirts and blazers—doodled in notebooks or read. He heard someone whisper at the back of the class and Sister Juanita looked up as the whispering stopped. He felt like shaking his head as he looked at his classmates. He wasn't really close to any of them. They seemed so . . . silly, though that really wasn't a good word. It was just that Lewis had it all planned, knew exactly where he was going, and these kids were satisfied with what they had, happy at the thought of living in North Manchester the rest of their lives.

But not Lewis, he thought. As long as he could remember he had always gotten A's in English and he was counting on that to take him places after high school and college. He wanted to be a newspaper reporter, talk to governors and astronauts, presidents and criminals, and see his name on the front page of a big newspaper. This summer one of his cousins in Rhode Island had gotten him a job as a copy boy at the Providence *Journal*. Mom hadn't been so crazy about the idea of his spending a summer away from home, but Dad thought it was great. A summer working at a real newspaper, watching the giant presses roll out newspapers still damp with ink, and knowing the people who put those words on paper. It seemed like a dream.

The final bell rang and he mechanically put the report card in the center of his history book and went out to the hallway, picking up his corduroy coat along the way. Yep, a dream all right. F, F, F. Once his parents saw that, so long summer job. And who knew if Cousin Paul would be able to arrange that copy boy job again.

His hands felt grimy from handling the report card so he went to the basement, where the lavatories were. The boys' bathroom was empty and he washed his hands in one of the large, dirty porcelain sinks. Over the sinks were large windows cranked open with a hand wheel, and the center one was open. In spite of it all he smiled at the sight. Poor Mr. Flaherty still hadn't gotten that window fixed, despite how many complaints from Sister Alicia, the principal.

The basement of the school held storage rooms, the nurse's office, a jumble of old desks and chairs, and the boiler room, where Mr. Flaherty held court. Lewis stopped outside the boiler room, jacket slung over one arm. The door was open and along a short brick-lined hallway was a row of trashcans. One of the prized chores in school was dumping the classroom wastebaskets because it meant a trip to the boiler room and a chance to talk to Mr. Flaherty. And if he was in a good mood, he'd let you dump the trash right into the incinerator, which was at the end of the brick hallway. That door was also open and Lewis watched the roaring of the flames and the red and orange glow of the coals. That must be what Hell looks like, he thought. Spending forever there, with the coals against your skin, burning and burning.

Mr. Flaherty stepped out from his workroom, which led off from the hallway. He wore dark green chino workpants and shirt, and his hands were browned and permanently stained with grease. He was almost completely bald and his black-rimmed glasses were held together with masking tape.

Before he spoke Lewis could smell him, smell the thick odor of mouthwash. "You need something?" he demanded.

Mr. Flaherty was not in a good mood. Lewis thought

quickly for a moment and said, "The window in the boys' bathroom still won't close."

The janitor snorted in distaste. "That nun principal send you down on that? Let me tell you, kiddo, bad enough I spent twelve years learning from the likes of her, now I have to work for her, too. Now you run along, 'fore I take a hand to you."

He ran along.

At home his older brother Earl had left a note, saying he would be out with friends that night. Drinking, no doubt. Lewis didn't care. Their parents wouldn't be back until tomorrow.

He rambled through the empty house and in the kitchen he ate some chocolate chip cookies and drank a glass of milk. He sat on a high wooden stool and through the kitchen window he watched the sun set out beyond the dull brown hills that ringed North Manchester. Occasionally he glanced over at the small wall clock and checked the time. Five p.m. Six ten p.m. Six thirty p.m. The minutes were sliding away. He looked over at the counter where Mom made her Italian dinners and pizza or fish every Friday night. The dull white report card sat in the middle of the counter, mocking him

Maybe, he thought, maybe we could tell Mom and Dad we lost the report card. Or the nuns couldn't find it and would give him a new one on Monday. It might work.

He slapped his hands with disgust on the counter and walked out the back door to the rear lawn. Sure. It'd work. But only for a couple of days. And what would those be like? Skulking around the house, wondering if his parents believed him, wondering if maybe they'd call up the convent to complain or double-check. And then it would be worse, much worse, if they found out that deceit.

Lewis sat down on the stone steps and drew up his knees to

his chin. He felt like he was six. He was panicking, his chin was trembling, and his eyes were teary. And over what? An ink mark on a piece of cardboard. That was all. He took a deep, shuddering breath, and thought, yeah, that's all. He imagined Mom and Dad coming home tomorrow. Looking at the report card. The tense looks. The yelling. Maybe even a slap or two across the face. Then the phone calls. One to the school, demanding to know how he screwed up. And one to Cousin Paul, canceling the summer job. All because of one lousy mark.

The night air was still warm, strange for March. Stars were starting to appear against the dark sky and the color reminded him of Sister Juanita's habit. He recalled how she reached into her bottom desk drawer, pulling out the blank report cards and filling in those marks, and he remembered wondering, which one of those will be mine. Which one of those will bear that damnable F. He shook his head and tightened his grip on his knees, and the smell of the school soap on his hands made him think of something, of something in the boys' bathroom, and in a very few minutes he had locked the house and was walking back into town.

This sure is crazy, he thought, huddled against the cold brick of St. Mary's High School. And all because of algebra. Something about it never clicked with him. He could understand numbers all right, multiplication and division and fractions. But letters instead of numbers? X's and Y's? It was like part of his brain was dead, that it couldn't even begin to grasp the meaning or basic function of algebra. So he had gone from a B to a C and now, that blasted F.

The wind picked up, stirring dust and dead leaves from last year around his feet. He was at the rear of the school, in the fenced-in asphalt lot where gym and recess were held. In front of him were three windows, and the middle one moved easily enough in his hands. All he had to do was swing himself in, put his feet on the bathroom sink, and he'd be in. Clipped to his belt was an old Boy Scout flashlight. And then . . .

He turned around again. God, can I do this? Will I go to Hell? Not only are we trespassing, we're stealing and lying. Because inside the school was Sister Juanita's desk, and it would be easy enough, yes, so easy, to steal a blank one and forge a new card. One with a C in algebra instead of an F. Forge it and give it to his parents tomorrow, apologize for not doing better. Get some good-natured kidding from Dad, and on Sunday, forge Dad's signature on the real card, pass it in, and start working like the Devil himself to do better next semester.

Against the brick wall his hands were trembling. It was very dark and there had been hardly any traffic on the short walk to the school. Up and over. That's all it would take. Or face parents tomorrow with the real thing, and spend a summer here instead of Rhode Island. He tried deep breathing to calm the trembling but instead it made his head dizzy. Such a small town. It only took a few minutes to walk from one end to another, and it wasn't for him. He imagined living in a big city, bigger than Manchester or Boston, where it was hard to sleep at night because of the traffic and the music. He wanted that so bad it was almost something he could grab. He closed his eyes and tried to imagine Hell again, the burning coals and fire, but all he saw was the red of the mark. F.

He flipped down the window and clambered inside, reaching out with his feet to the sink. His feet flailed in the empty air and he started sliding on his stomach on the window, banging his chin in the process, and he bit his tongue. He almost cried out, imagining falling to the cement floor and breaking a leg, but one foot touched the sink and in a few seconds he was there.

The bathroom was dark and there was a sharp odor of chemicals. Mr. Flaherty must've cleaned it before leaving. He touched the flashlight on his belt and rubbed at his chin. A scratch was there, one that stung, and he looked up at the window. Could he make it back up there when he was done? He touched the cold porcelain of the sink. He'd have to. There was nothing else left. In the lavatory another sink was dripping, the loud noise sounding like a series of gunshots.

He stood at the doorway, wondering why his legs were shaking so. This is stupid, he thought. We've been down here dozens of times, hell, *hundreds* of times before. Why the shaking legs? Why the dry mouth which wouldn't go away? Why did his hands itch, as if they wanted a gun or a club to hold? To his right were the stairs and to the left were the piles of furniture, storage rooms, and the boiler room. God, I'm so scared, and it was because of the time and place. During the day when there was light and hundreds of other kids here, the school seemed to be alive. Now it was so dark it almost hurt his eyes to squint, and the only sounds were from dripping water and the occasional creak or groan from the pipes.

Can a school be haunted?

Lewis started up the stairs, a hand gliding along the cold metal of the banister. He noticed the dusty smell of the school—the dirt, the chalk dust, the sweat from all the kids roaming around during the day. The stairs were gritty from dirt and he was halfway up the first flight when the noise made him freeze and grab onto the banister with both hands.

Below him a door had slammed.

He forced himself to look. Below and at the other end of the basement a red glowing light was coming out of an open door, and the banister was sweaty in his hands as he tried to imagine what was there. A fire? The Devil? Some footsteps echoed out and the door closed, and he heard muttered cursing as Mr. Flaherty stepped out and slowly walked up the other stairs. Oh Lord, Lewis thought. Mr. Flaherty's still here and he's drunk. And he had heard whispered stories out in the playground about Mr. Flaherty's temper when he was drunk. He tried not to move but his arms were shaking as he watched Mr. Flaherty ascend the other stairs, his way lit by streetlights from outside. Lewis let out a breath of air when he heard another slam. The door outside. Mr. Flaherty must be outside. That's all.

The lavatory was still there, with the open window that led out. And out there was a real report card, with a real failing grade. He started back up the stairs.

At the first floor corridor he saw he didn't need his flashlight. The outside streetlights lit up enough of the interior but when he started up the hallway, hugging close to the wall, something struck his face and he stopped, listening to a clattering noise that seemed to go on forever. He reached up and touched a swinging coat hanger which his head had struck. *Idiot,* he thought. *Let's make some more noise.* He waited a few more minutes and then kept on going down the hallway, but this time he stayed in the middle. His heart was pounding so hard he couldn't make out the individual beats. The sound was one giant roar that filled his ears.

The door to Sister Juanita's classroom was partially opened and he slowly opened it farther, the creaking of the hinges echoing in the room. The room and the rows of desks seemed smaller in the nighttime, less real, like it was all a bad dream. Sister Juanita's desk was in the far corner, the American flag next to it, and the blackboards seemed like polished stone in the faint light. His chest felt as if it was going to burst and he licked his dry lips as he walked across the classroom floor. At every step a floorboard creaked.

At the desk he wondered what Sister Juanita might do if she found him here. If she came in right now, habit swishing and flowing, the rosary beads clicking, switching on the overhead lights. What would she do? Grab him by the hair, no doubt, and hit him a few times. Call home and maybe speak to his older brother Earl, or even demand the phone number of his aunt and uncle in Rhode Island. He wiped his hands on his jacket and leaned forward, not quite believing he was actually going to go through Sister Juanita's desk. It was stealing.

But his hand moved forward anyway, touching the polished wood of the lower desk handle. He tugged at it and the drawer wouldn't budge. He tugged again, harder, and then knelt down and used both hands.

Damn! He sank forward on his knees. The drawer was locked. He jerked at it a few times, his hands finally slipping off the handle in the effort. It was locked, and he had done all of this for nothing. Tomorrow he was still going to be dead. This time he sat down against the desk and drew up his knees and cried into his hands, muffling the tears with his coatsleeve, the musty smell no comfort at all.

In a while he was done, his face dried, his eyes watery and aching from the sharp sting of his tears. He was about to get up and slink downstairs when he tried to remember one thing, what Sister Juanita did every morning. She would sweep into class and nod at the kids, her books and ledger in her gnarled hands, and then she'd sit down, open the center desk drawer, and then . . .

Still on his knees, he moved over to the center drawer, pushing her swivel chair out of the way. He tugged at the center drawer and it slid easily out, and from inside the desk there was a click, as a mechanism of some sort was released. He tried again with the lower drawer and it came out with no problem at all.

The flashlight was in his hands and the strong light made him blink. Inside the drawer were pencils, pens, an ink pad, two black-board erasers, a pile of envelopes, and there, almost at the bottom and bound with an elastic band, the blank report cards. His prize. He gently pulled one free and replaced everything in the drawer, and then closed both drawers shut, also moving the swivel chair back. He put the blank report card down his shirt, and even though it was cold and scratchy on his skin, it felt wonderful. He was going to make it.

And he was halfway out of the classroom when the voice came.

"Hey, you! Stop that!"

He closed his eyes. Caught. He couldn't move, waiting for the hand on his shoulder, the slap on the face, the fingers tugging at his ear. The failure and now all of this. He should have stayed home, for what could he ever do now? He started praying but instead of the formal Hail Mary or Our Father, he just said, Oh Lord, over and over.

The voice came again, louder. "Stop that, now!" He opened his eyes. He was still alone in the room. The voice was coming from outside. Without knowing why he was doing so, he walked over to the row of windows, just above the bright gray of the radiator. One window was still open and he looked down through the screen, at the fenced-in yard where he had been a hundred hours ago. The corner streetlight cast an odd glow over the asphalt and Mr. Flaherty was there, a bottle in one hand, his other hand raised. He wasn't alone. Two young men were in front of him, laughing and poking at him with their hands. They had long hair and both wore dungaree

31

jackets. Lewis held his breath. No one could see them from the street. Only Lewis was watching. Mr. Flaherty tried to stumble away and the men were with him.

One said, "C'mon, Curt, grab the bum's wallet and let's screw."

Mr. Flaherty turned. "No, you won't," and he brought the bottle down on Curt's shoulder. The young man yelped and cursed and Lewis bit his lip, trying not to scream, trying not to cry out. Suddenly Mr. Flaherty was sitting on the asphalt, his legs splayed out both hands clasped to his chest.

"Here," the young man said, reaching out with a hand, the streetlight glittering sharply on what was there, and he punched Mr. Flaherty twice in the chest again. He coughed and in an instant the two men were running away, heading for the street. They both turned in unison, as if they were brothers, and looked back at Mr. Flaherty, self-satisfied grins on their young faces.

Lewis held onto the wooden windowsill with both hands, not moving. Below him Mr. Flaherty sat on the asphalt, stock still, hands at his chest. Then Mr. Flaherty started weaving slightly, from side to side, and he slowly rolled over to the hard surface of the asphalt, as if he was suddenly exhausted. A leg twitched, and then he was still.

Out on the deck later that night I sat and looked out at the stars, and I tried not to look at the back yard, which fell towards the slow moving Bellamy River. I tried to keep my gaze up at the stars, trying to remember the constellations, but like so many things I failed at it. My right hand throbbed with a dull ache where an emergency room doctor had cleaned and stitched my wound. There was a taste of dead ashes in my mouth, despite the half-drunk bottle of beer in my hand. What Annie had said brought it all back.

I never mentioned it to anyone, not even the police. How could I explain what I was doing in school at that time of the night? The forgery had gone on, I had gotten that summer job and others, and I had gotten here, to where I wanted to go so bad. But it never had been like I had planned. At some points in my life, like my high school and college graduations, at my first newspaper job and the time I won a journalism award two years ago, I could never quite enjoy what I had achieved. It was always spoiled by the thought of how I had gotten there, over the corpse of Mr. Flaherty. At those times when I was supposed to be happy, and when I had a little too much to drink, I always imagined I saw someone just stepping out of a door, or ducking behind a group of people. And this someone would always be wearing faded green chinos.

Annie came out, sitting next to me, a soft hand on my shoulder. "You okay?"

"Not bad," I said, trying to keep my tone light. "We ought to call your Aunt Mary and complain about those glasses."

"Maybe so," she said, and her voice was low.

We sat there for some minutes, until I couldn't stand it any more, and I said, "What did Mom say about my report card? She never mentioned it to me, not ever."

Annie shrugged her shoulders. "She told me at my bridal shower that you were her best-behaved son, except for that report card your freshman year. Some nun had talked to her at a school function, congratulating her on making you work harder. I guess you went from an F to a B in one semester."

Which was true. "That's right."

"And that was the first time she had ever heard about it, but by that time you were in Rhode Island and she never bothered to bring it up. Your mom gave me the idea she thought it was kinda funny."

My throat was dry, despite the beer. Kinda funny. "Oh."

She touched my shoulder again, a soft flicker. "What happened, back then? It really bothered you, didn't it?"

I looked over at Annie and thought, well, maybe it's time to tell someone what happened back then. Maybe it was time to stop the lies. In her eyes I saw a look of love and concern, and I knew it was for a man she thought she knew everything about. And what would my wife then think, if she knew how I stood there and watched a man bleed to death, for a report card mark? I had wanted a wife like Annie all my days, but some secrets would always have to stay secrets.

"What's wrong?" she softly asked again.

The night air seemed cooler and my hand still ached.

"Nothing," I said, lying for the first time as a married man. I took a drink from my beer and looked down at the bushes and the yard out beyond the deck, and in the darkness I thought I saw someone move.

With five brothers, many of my stories involve the relationships among brothers. There's a bond there, of course, but many times there is competition, old resentments, and in this story, deadly secrets.

Not Much of a Trade

Ross had once lived in Tegucigalpa, and between jobs he would pass the hours by walking along the dusty streets, past the lame dogs scuffling in piles of garbage and the children, always tagging after him, their dirty brown hands open in beseechment. In Cancun, he had a villa only a few minutes away from the beach, and from the second-floor balcony he could see the pale blue of the Caribbean, though he always looked toward the streets, at the dark-green buses trundling toward the hotel zone, packed with hotel workers who stared impassively out at the sea.

Now Ross lived in a wooden cottage on a lake in Conner, New Hampshire. The water of the lake was cold and deep blue. The lake was called Piscataqua, a name from the Algonquins, who had lived there for thousands of years, until a pale race arrived in leaking boats from the ocean and burned them out.

His cottage was built on a small point of land that jutted into the lakewater. The land was hilly and fell away at the rear to a dirt road that led to Conner. On some days, while clearing away brush or mowing the lawn with a handmower, he wondered what would have happened if the Algonquins had had muskets, if they and the other Indian tribes had had an effective confederation, a good intelligence system. If they

35

had met every landing with muskets and axes, would the boats have stopped? Perhaps. But then again, he always rooted for the underdog, which explained his Red Sox T-shirts.

On this night, Ross ambled out to the rear porch and sat in an old wicker chair. He listened to music from the state's only classical station, from Concord, and sipped at whiskey and lake water. The whiskey was Jameson's. Rocking in the chair, he watched the sun set in gold and red into the distant mountains and watched the lake darken. The lake was mostly clear of boats. Tourists hadn't discovered it quite yet, though there were cottages here and there. Listening to the hoarse cry of the loons, he remembered his older brother Sam saying it was the cry of the old Indians, crying out their dismay at what had happened to the world. It was a good story. He wished it was true.

This was his home state, and Sam—though Ross hadn't seen him in years—lived only a few towns away. All around the world and back to New Hampshire. He was sure the staff psychiatrists would love that one, though he had no intention of ever seeing them again. He listened to the night sounds and rocked in the chair, feeling the old wounds ache.

Peaceful, but not peaceful enough. He finished his drink and went to work cleaning his guns.

The smell of the gun oil always brought back memories. Of those cool October nights, sitting by the fireplace with Sam, cleaning their deer rifles before the hunting season started. Basic training, and the D.I. hammering him and the other scared recruits as they cleaned and recleaned their automatic weapons. A long, rainy weekend in Vienna, holed up in a pension and waiting for a signal, cleaning his weapons to hide his boredom and fear.

He cleaned his pistols and his revolvers and his shotguns,

and even his old deer rifle, but he never touched a weapon of his that was hidden away back in the loft. It was a complex weapon, with a scope and extended magazine and beefed-up slings, and his feelings for the weapon were just as complex . . .

Ross had once lived a time when things were due yesterday, of flights missed and trains caught just in time. Sleeping and waking in strange hotel rooms, always feeling out of sync, not sure what was going on and where to go, only knowing that quiet men in suits would point him in the right direction. He always carried a large black case with him and at night he would sleep with it nearby, the case fastened to his arm by a thin chain.

Now the days were long, filled only with decisions of when to weed the garden and when to recaulk the boat, of when to drive into Conner and get some kerosene. The nightmares and bad dreams, usually colored in red, didn't come as often, but when sleeping at night his right wrist always itched and ached, and he knew the chain was still there.

His only friend was Tyler, the postman, who drove through the backwoods of Conner delivering mail and gossip. Ross was out behind his cottage, clearing away some brush and saplings, using a small hand axe and saw. He had stripped off his T-shirt and was wearing only workboots and khaki pants. His .45 caliber pistol was strapped to his waist and his upper body was tanned except for the odd white patches and lumps that scarred his skin.

When Tyler's rusty blue Ford station wagon rumbled to a stop near the mailbox, Ross put down his tools and walked over, drying the sweat off his hands with his T-shirt. Tyler was a short old man, completely bald, who always smoked unfiltered Camels. A blue magnetic sign on his car said U.S.

Mail in white letters. He nodded to Tyler and the man nodded back, handing over a bundle of fliers and magazines fastened together with elastic bands.

"Here you go, Ross. There's not much there. You don't get any letters, do you? Not much except your magazines."

"I'm not the letter-writing type."

Tyler tapped the ashes off his cigarette and they fell on his grey shirt. "That's a damn shame. The more people like you write, the better business we get, and I can get myself a raise. I'll be coming back again next Tuesday if you're here. Need anything?"

"Some milk and bacon, if you can."

Ross reached into his pants and Tyler held up a wrinkled hand. "You can get me on the flip side, don't worry about it." He took another drag off his cigarette. "Something else you might be worrying about."

An old, familiar tingling tugged at Ross's neck. "Oh? Property taxes going up again?"

"You should wish. Couple of out-of-staters been nosing around looking for you, asking questions."

"They ask for me specifically?" Ross asked, his voice level.

"Nope. But then again, Ross, there ain't many guys of your age living alone around here, especially one with so many scars as you got." Tyler eyed him. "You've been in some spats in your time, haven't you?"

"Spats is a good word."

"Fair enough. You in trouble with the government or something?"

Ross looked down at his mail. "Could be. I sort of left the people I worked for without saying goodbye."

Tyler chuckled. "Reminds me of what I did back in North Africa during the war. Left for a whorehouse without properly saying goodbye and got some time in the stockade."

38

Tyler looked up and winked at him. "But it was worth it. Listen here, you need some help or something?"

"No, not really."

"Then keep watch. I think you'll be getting some visitors soon. More's the pity, 'cause I enjoy talking to you. Now I gotta get going, I'm wasting money. You take care."

Ross waited until the station wagon was out of sight down the dusty road and then he went up to the house.

Well, he thought. *About time.*

Inside the cottage, he flipped through the mail, looking again for a letter from his brother Sam, though he knew that was foolish. Sam didn't know he was here. Sam probably didn't even know he was back in the States. But Ross had faith in his brother and he had a feeling that somehow Sam would find out through his sources that he was back. Ross could call him, of course, but that would be too dangerous. He didn't want to drag Sam into this, even though he wanted to talk to his older brother. He threw the mail down on the kitchen table.

"Stuck again, right?" he said aloud. He was hot and sweaty from outside and he took a cold Molson's from the refrigerator and went out to sit on the front porch. He drank the crisp beer, the water beading down his wrist, and watched some water-skiers crisscross the lake, sending up spouts of foam. From the corner of the porch he could see down to the driveway. Some more brush to clear. Got to clear the field. Fields of fire. He stood there, letting the breeze coming up from the lake cool him. He remembered one of the last times he had talked to his brother.

It had been right after his stint in the service, when, thanks to his shooting skills, he had been offered his new job. He had been drinking beer with Sam up at his farm in Pierce. They were in the kitchen and Sam's wife Maddy was in the kids' bedrooms, trying to get them to stop squawking. The brothers had talked about past fights and arguments, past stories and deeds. Ross saw that Sam, even though he wasn't yet thirty, had deep lines around his eyes and his hands were squat and rough. Sam worked the farm during the day and drove a delivery truck at night.

"Remember the time we stole those apples from Mr. Pope's farm?" Sam asked. "And how he sent some buckshot after us and nearly had a heart attack?"

"Yeah," Ross said. "Dad almost croaked from that one."

Maddy came into the kitchen, frowned at the collection of empty beer bottles on the table, and then went into the living room. She had swelled with weight in the years Ross had known her, and her face was red and worn.

"You know," Ross continued, "I remember when you told us you were getting married. What a mess. You were eighteen and I knew Dad wanted you to go to college. What made you do that in such a hurry? Love?"

Ross had been smiling, but when he saw the look on his brother's face the smile slipped away.

Sam said, "What makes you think I had a choice?"

"Hunh?"

Sam gave him a sour grin and picked up his beer. "Little brother, you sure can be dumb sometimes. Your nephew Solomon was born in August. Remember what month Maddy and I got married?"

"March. But I remember Ma saying Solomon was premature."

Sam shook his head. "Yeah, that was true. Solomon was premature, but only by a week. C'mon, Ross, she and the kid came home only a couple of days later. No, love didn't make me do it in such a hurry."

From the bedroom off the kitchen, Solomon screaming, and was soon joined by the twin girls. S..... frowned.

"Remember this, bro—whatever you do in life, make sure you do it right, 'cause it'll follow you forever."

"Hey," Maddy shouted from the living room, "they're your kids, too, Sam! Make 'em shut up!"

Sam got up and said, "You know, in high school I got straight A's in math. Straight A's. And I threw that all away for a few steamy nights. Not much of a trade."

True, Ross thought now, *not much of a trade.*

He finished his Molson's and watched the speedboats. *I got travel and money and job security, brother, and I threw away a lot more. A lot more.*

He came to love the lake and the cottage after being there only a couple of years. He never tired of watching how the seasons changed the lake. In spring, after the ice growled and broke away, buds would sprout on the trees and the birds would come back, crying almost in joy, it seemed, when they nestled in around the lake. In the fall, those same birds would quietly gather up and fly south, and the reds and oranges along the shoreline made it look like the lake was ablaze.

In the winter, snow cloaked everything in a white silence and he would ski out on the frozen surface, the squeak-squeak of the bindings and the skis cutting through the snow the only sound. On those trips, he would see tracks in the snow, and after a while he could recognize the tiny pads that meant rabbit and the cloven shapes that meant deer. Sometimes he'd follow the tracks just to see where they led, and in a way it was important to see where they hid.

Summer meant warm evenings on the porch sipping whiskey and water, reading old history books, and thinking a lot—and rowing among the inlets and islands around the lake, the oars cutting swiftly and surely through the water. At night he liked to ship the oars, lie back on a blanket in the boat, and look up at the stars, letting the boat drift with the wind. Up there the stars were bright and crowded, almost too intense to look at, and he would gaze at them for hours, sometimes seeing the swift-moving dot of light that meant a satellite.

A military satellite, most likely. Reconnaissance or God knows what. Even out here he couldn't escape them. Disturbed at the sight, he would take up the oars and slowly go home.

One night he awoke suddenly, the sheets wrapped around him, the room stuffy and hot. He tried to remember what he had dreamed, but he couldn't. He got out of bed and walked over to the window, looking at the moonlight dance on the lake water. Secrets. So many of them. He remembered the last time with Sam.

He had come home on leave, tanned and sure of what he was doing. It must have been his first year. Sam and he hadn't had many secrets until then. Sam had told him about the time he got caught shoplifting at Weekum's and Ross had told him about the first time he had started to become intimate with a girl. But this time they had gone up to an apple grove on a small hill near Sam's farm and had sat down on a stone wall. It had been fall—Ross remembered their feet crunching on the fall leaves.

"Well," Sam had said, "there's the family farm—though God knows the bank owns most of it."

"Looks good, Sam."

Sam had glanced over at him, a sharp look on his face. "What have you been up to, Ross?"

"Oh, this and that."

"Come on, Ross, I mean working. What are you doing for work?"

Ross tried to make light of it. "Oh, a business down south. We do some government contracts, private stuff. Not very interesting."

"Yeah, but I'm interested. What do you do?"

Ross had stared out at the farm, wishing they were talking baseball. "Management work."

Sam said, "This is your older brother talking, Ross, and I don't like the line you're feeding me. I asked a simple question. What exactly do you do for a living?"

The air felt cold on his face. "I can't tell you," he'd said, and a nasty image came to him of a Frenchman in Marseilles, in a fine suit, looking up in horror as his white shirt was suddenly stained red.

Sam got up. "Well, you're still my brother by blood, but I can't see you as a good brother in my book, for all that. So forget it, Ross—forget I ever asked you an important thing."

Ross had followed Sam back to the farmhouse but the weekend was ruined, and the very few letters he got from Sam after that were brief and dull, and they had never spoken together again.

The following day, he went fishing and didn't catch a thing. When he returned to the cottage he saw a man on his dock. Parker.

The man was in his early forties and dressed in a black two-piece suit and a light-blue shirt with a black tie. His hair was blond and cut short. He lifted a hand in greeting as Ross cut the engine and let the boat drift into the dock.

Ross nodded and tied off the boat, then started walking up to the cottage, not bothering to see if Parker was following him. Inside, he grabbed a Molson's and stared out the kitchen window. A black sedan was parked back by the mailbox, and it was empty. Ross peered some and saw a man standing near the grove of trees to the right, and another up on the ridge. They both wore suits and sunglasses—he knew what they carried under their suit coats. He took a long swallow of the beer and didn't taste a thing. The porch door opened and Parker came in.

"No, thanks," Parker said, noticing the beer. "Can't drink while on duty."

"I didn't offer you one."

Parker smiled. "So you didn't."

He went out to the porch and sat in the wicker chair. Parker followed and leaned against a porch railing. Behind Parker was a rolled-up blind, which moved in the breeze.

"You're here," Ross said. "What do you want?"

Parker held out his fine, soft hands. "We want you."

"Suppose I don't want to go."

"It doesn't really matter what you want, does it? You had an agreement with us and you broke that by running out."

"I didn't run. I flew."

"Whatever. You didn't hide that well, did you? We were expecting plastic surgery, maybe a voice change, or even a bald head—but, nope, you're just the same. We've had camera crews in these godforsaken woods for the past week watching you, and let me tell you, Ross, I never knew a man could waste so much time weeding a garden and cutting trees. I would think you'd be so bored you'd call us up, begging to come back."

This time Ross tasted the beer. "I don't want to come back. Parker, there must be dozens of young, eager prospects you fellows can recruit. You can go out and peddle your line about fighting terrorism and promoting democracy from the end of a barrel and a 7.62 mm round. I bought it once—why don't you find some other suckers and leave me be?"

Parker folded his arms and sighed. "Except we've got something going on in Central America that needs our attention, and you're our best, Ross, you really are. Nobody else even comes close. But look at you. You're getting fat and lazy. I've read your reports, I know the stuff you've gone through, the weeks you've lived in the jungle on the run. Could you do that now? I doubt it. Not with the job you've made of concealing yourself."

Ross half watched a water-skier. "Why would I bother to hide? I knew you'd track me here sooner or later."

Parker scratched at a perfect cheek. "You know, they still talk about you in D.C.—the man who left without a word. Why did you leave so quick? Something about your last assignment?"

His last assignment. A two-day trip to Kenya. Routine, but just one more bloody chore.

"No. I realized that when I got up in the morning to shave I couldn't look at myself in the mirror."

Parker smiled. "So grow a beard."

"I like shaving. I didn't like the job any more."

Parker glanced at his wristwatch, and stood. "Enough, then. Here it is. We'll be by tomorrow at noon to pick you up and whatever stuff you need. A few weeks of retraining and then we're off to the south."

A breeze came across the porch, but it didn't cool him. "Suppose I do go?" Ross said. "Suppose I go and instead of taking out the enemy, I send a round over his head? Or suppose I take out a friend instead?"

Parker stood a distance from the porch railing and looked out at the lake. "Accidents can happen, Ross, you've been with us long enough to know that. Accidents of the worst kind. Like a house fire—a house fire where a guy named Sam lives with his wife and three kids. Understand? A house fire if you come and screw it up, a house fire if you don't come. I don't have the time to fool with you any more, Ross. It's been a nice talk but we've got business to attend to. I'll see you to-morrow. At noon."

After Parker left, he sat for a long time in the chair watching the sun, feeling the minutes and hours slip away. Why didn't we do better? he thought. Go up to Canada. Alaska. Change our face. Our look. Anything. Now Sam is threatened. Now what?

The sky grew darker, a deep shade of blue.

He had come here, he then decided, not to hide but to wait for Parker and his friends to come back. Because he wanted them to. Because he wanted to finish it, he wanted to stop it all. Stop hiding. Start something else.

Start running maybe?

Maybe.

The next morning, he got up with the sun, making a quick breakfast of a fried egg and three strips of bacon. A low mist clung to the ground and to the near shore, a faint rippling mass of white. In the upstairs loft, he rummaged around in the cardboard boxes and came back down carrying a small leather case in his hands. He put on a heavy wool sweater and went out to the small barn behind the cottage where his old pickup truck was parked. The engine started on the third try and he went down the dirt road, heading to Conner, knowing that unseen eyes were watching him, taking pictures and making recordings.

That early in the morning, Conner looked like a dead town, like a deserted Hollywood movie set. Hardly anything stirred, except for Polly's Place just out on the state road, which was crowded with parked cars. There was a State Police cruiser there and he imagined himself walking in and saying to the trooper, "Excuse me, sir, but there are some men threatening me—and the funny thing is, you and I pay their salaries."

He still hadn't forgotten the route, making the turns when they came up, traveling along old town roads, the truck bouncing over the potholes. At some point he was on a dirt road deep in the woods of Pierce, and he pulled his truck over near a streambed. It was the right place. His memory hadn't failed him.

Ross wondered if he was being followed. Probably, but with what? He hadn't noticed any traffic behind him. He rolled down the side window. Some early-morning birds chirped. The engine creaked as it cooled and then he heard the low thumping of a helicopter. He was sure there was a tracking device hidden somewhere in the pickup, but he didn't care.

He got out of the truck and went into the woods, carrying the leather case in his hands, following the streambed. The ground was spongy and moist, and he heard animals burrow away or run as he went deeper among the trees. *Don't worry, friends,* he thought, *today is someone else's hunting day.*

The ground rose and the trees thinned out, and he was at the crest of a hill. Below him, clear land fell away until it reached a farm, a two-story house with an attached barn, and he saw a thin curl of woodsmoke reach toward the sky. The sun was warmer and he pulled off his sweater, lowering himself to the ground, opening the leather case, and pulling out a pair of government-issue binoculars. Stolen, of course.

He brought the binoculars up to his eyes.

So. Sam must be doing well. There was a new truck in the back yard, this year's model. Ross scanned the house. The sunlight was reflecting off the windows and he couldn't see in. What was Sam doing? Clumping around the house, getting breakfast, talking to his wife Maddy about the kids or bills? Did a part of him ever wonder, hey, what's Ross doing now? Did he think about Ross at all? The back door slapped open and a tall boy came out, slouched over, wearing a leather jacket and jeans. Look at that—his nephew Solomon, so tall after all these years. The boy went into the barn and emerged a few moments later, wheeling a motorbike, which he jumped on and started up.

At the sound of the engine, the door opened again and there was Maddy, shaking her finger at Solomon. The boy shrugged his shoulders and drove off. Poor Maddy.

Two young girls then dove out the door and ran past Maddy. The twins, Jennifer and Janice. Pretty soon they'd be young women, probably even tougher to handle than Solomon. Ross shifted on the ground, the earth cool against his chest. He took away the binoculars and rubbed his eyes, and when he looked again his brother was in the yard.

Sam was stockier around the shoulders and the waist, but he still looked the same. Ross focused the glasses and his brother's face came in sharper. A lot more wrinkles, a lot more worries. God, the questions I'd like to ask you, bro. What you've been doing. How the farm's going. Have you gotten over your disappointments, Sam? Have you forgotten all the math you learned in school, the math you thought was going to take you places?

The glasses trembled in his hands. *Well, why not?* he thought. *Let's do it. Let's get up here and walk down.* Sam will look up from his chores and glance up at the hill— He'd love to see the look on his brother's face as he got closer.

Surprise, probably. Then shock. Then—

Then *what?* Happiness? Anger? Puzzlement?

Sam would start asking questions, and right then he had

an urge to tell it all. To sit down with Sam and tell him every-thing, like he'd done so many times before. Sam, he would say, you're not going to believe this, but I kill other people for a living. It's what I do and what I get paid for. And if I don't keep on doing it they're going to hurt you and Maddy and the kids.

And Sam would say, No way they would, Ross, we'll take care of them.

Sure. Right. Sam would probably glare at him and say, Why did you come here, then? Why are you putting us in danger? And Sam would be right. Why *had* he come there?

Why? Because he'd always gone to his older brother when he was in trouble, that's why. He looked again through the binoculars. Sam was working on the engine of the truck. Probably changing the oil himself to save a few bucks. Off in the distance, Ross could hear the helicopter. And he knew he wouldn't go down.

He got up and went back into the woods, the glasses dan-gling from the strap in his hand.

Later that morning, he cleaned the house and packed some belongings in a knapsack, which he put out on the back porch. He set a small fire in the woodstove and burned some of his papers, then he went out and checked on his boat.

Back on the porch, the sunlight was streaming through and he pulled the bamboo blinds closed. When he caught his breath, he went upstairs to the loft and found, where he'd hidden it far back, a long black case.

He took it gingerly back downstairs and spent the next hour cleaning and putting the weapon together, adjusting the slings and the scope. The smell of the oil was strong in his nostrils, but this time it brought no memories.

What *would* have happened if the Algonquins had killed

those early settlers? What *would* have happened if he had told Parker back then, when he was just getting out of the service, that he wasn't interested? What then?

He looked around the cottage. It was such a peaceful place, but he hadn't brought much peace here. Not with his past. And it was no longer time to hide out.

Watch what you do, Sam had said. It'll follow you the rest of your life.

Carrying the sniper's rifle, he went out to the porch. The noon sun was making tiny squares of light on the hardwood floor. He drew the wicker chair close to the side blind, and with a pocketknife he cut away a small square of the fabric.

From across the lake came the sound of the noon whistle from the Conner Volunteer Fire Department. Ross's breathing was now regular and slow. He checked again that his knapsack was by the rear door. From the door to the boat, at a dead run, would only take a minute.

A car approached the cottage. He took another deep breath, raised the rifle to his shoulder, and sighted in on the mailbox. A clear field of fire. The black sedan came to a halt. No more time to hide—time to run. He wondered if Parker had a brother who would have warned him. It'll follow you, it'll always follow you.

He worked the action. Parker stepped out, followed by the other men.

Ross took a deep breath and let it out halfway. Then he began squeezing the trigger. It was all he could do.

In writing this story, I had the idea of a stone-cold criminal who could turn vicious in a second, and who could also be the favorite uncle of his nieces and nephews, because of the gifts and attention he brought to them. A brother who did bad things, but also looked out for his family. For whatever reason, this story was a lot of fun to write.

The Necessary Brother

I still have the problem of last evening's phone call on my mind as I wait for Sarah to finish her shower this Thursday holiday morning in November. From my vantage point on the bed I see that the city's weather is overcast, and I wonder if snow flurries will start as I begin the long drive that waits for me later in the morning. The bedroom is large and is in the corner of the building, with a balcony that overlooks Central Park. I pause between the satin sheets and wait, my hands folded behind my head, as the shower stops and Sarah ambles out. She smiles at me and I smile back, feeling effortless in doing that, for we have no secrets from each other, no worries or frets about what the future may bring. That was settled months ago, in our agreement when we first met, and our arrangement works for both of us.

She comes over, toweling her long blonde hair with a thick white towel, smile still on her face, a black silk dressing gown barely covering her model's body. As she clambers on the bed and straddles me, she drops the towel and leans forward, enveloping me in her damp hair, nuzzling my neck.

"I don't see why you have to leave, Carl," she says, in her breathless voice that can still make my head turn. "And I can't believe you're driving. That must be at least four hours away. Why don't you fly?"

"It's more like five," I say, idly caressing her slim hips. "And I'm driving because flying is torture this time of year, and I want to travel alone."

She gently bites me on the neck and then sits back, her pale blue eyes laughing at me. With her long red fingernails she idly traces the scars along my side and chest, and then touches the faint ones on my arms where I had the tattoos removed years ago. When we first met and first made love, Sarah was fascinated by the marks on my body, and it's a fascination that has grown over the months. At night, during our loveplay, she will sometimes stop and touch a scar and demand a story, and sometimes I surprise her by telling her the truth.

"And why are you going?" she asks. "We could have a lot of fun here today, you and me. Order up a wonderful meal. Watch the parades and old movies. Maybe even catch one of the football games."

I reach up and stroke her chin. "I'm going because I have to. And because it's family."

She makes a face and gets out of bed, drawing the gown closer to her. "Hah. Family. Must be some family to make you drive all that way. But I don't understand you, not at all. You hardly ever talk about them, Carl. Not ever. What's the rush? What's the reason?"

I shrug. "Because they're family. No other reason."

Sarah tosses the towel at my head and says in a joking tone, "You're impossible, and I'm not sure why I put up with you."

"Me too," I say, and I get up and go into the steamy bathroom as she begins to dive into the walk-in closet that belongs to her.

★ ★ ★ ★ ★

I stay in the shower for what seems hours, luxuriating in the hot and steamy water, remembering the times growing up in Boston Falls when showers were rationed to five minutes apiece because of the creaky hot water that could only stand so much use every cold day. Father had to take his shower before going to the mills, and Brad was next because he was the oldest. I was fortunate, being in the middle, for our youngest brother, Owen, sometimes ended up with lukewarm water, if that. And Mother, well, we never knew when she bathed. It was a family secret.

I get out and towel myself down, enjoying the feel of the warm heat on my lean body as I enter the bedroom. Another difference. Getting out of the shower used to mean walking across cold linoleum, grit on your feet as you got dressed for school. Now it means walking into a warm and carpeted bedroom, my clothes laid out neatly on my bed. I dress quickly, knowing I will have to move fast to avoid the traffic for the day's parade. I go out to the kitchen overlooking the large and dark sunken living room, and Sarah is gone, having left breakfast for me on the marbletop counter. The day's *Times* is there, folded, and I stand and eat the scrambled eggs, toast, and bacon, while drinking a large glass of orange juice and a cup of coffee.

When I unfold the *Times* a note falls out. It's in Sarah's handwriting. *Do have a nice trip,* it says. *I've called down to Raphael. See you when you get back. Yours, S.*

Yours. Sarah has never signed a note or a letter to me that says love. Always it's "yours." That's because Sarah tells the truth.

I wash the dishes and go into the large walk-in closet near the door that leads out to the hallway. I select a couple of heavy winter jackets, and from a combination-lock box similar to a fuse box, take out a Bianchi shoulder holster, a 9mm Beretta, and two spare magazines. I slide on the holster and pull a wool cardigan on and leave and take the elevator down, whistling as I do so.

Out on the sidewalk by the lobby Raphael nods to me as I step out into the brisk air, his doorkeeper's uniform clean and sharp. My black Mercedes is already pulled up, engine purring, faint tendrils of exhaust eddying up into the thick, cold air. Raphael smiles and touches his cap with a brief salute. There is an old knife scar on his brown cheek, and though still a teenager, he has seen some things that could give me the trembling wake-ups at two a.m. In addition to his compensation from the building, I pay Raphael an extra hundred a week to keep his eyes open for me. The doorkeepers in this city open and close lots of doors, and they also open and close a lot of secrets, and that's a wonderful resource for my business.

Raphael walks with me and opens the door. "A cold morning, Mr. Curtis. Are you ready for your drive?"

I slip a folded ten-dollar bill into his white-gloved hand, and it disappears effortlessly. "Absolutely. Trunk packed?"

"That it is," he says as I toss the two winter coats onto the passenger's seat and buckle up in the warm interior. I always wear seat belts, a rule that, among others, I follow religiously. As he closes the door, Raphael smiles again and says, *"Vaya con Dios,"* and since the door is shut, I don't reply. But I do smile in return and he goes back to his post.

I'm about fifteen minutes into my drive when I notice the thermos bottle on the front seat, partially covered by the two coats I dumped there. At a long stoplight I unscrew the cap and smell the fresh coffee, then take a quick drink and decide Raphael probably deserves a larger Christmas bonus this year.

★ ★ ★ ★ ★

As I drive I listen to my collection of classical music CDs. I can't tell you the difference between an opus and a symphony, a quartet or a movement, or who came first, Bach or Beethoven. But I do know what I like, and classical music is something that just seems to settle into my soul, like hot honey traveling into a honeycomb. I have no stomach for, nor interest in, what passes as modern music. When I drive I start at one end of my CD collection and in a month or so I get to the other end, and then start again.

The scenery as I go through the busy streets and across the numbered highways on my way to Connecticut is an urban sprawl of dead factories, junkyards, tenements, vacated lots, and battered cars with bald tires. Not a single pedestrian I see looks up. They all stare at the ground, as if embarrassed at what is around them, as if made shy by what has become of their country. I'm not embarrassed. I'm somewhat amused. It's the hard lives in that mess that give me my life's work.

I drive on, humming along to something on the CD that features a lot of French horns.

Through Connecticut I drive in a half-daze, listening to the music, thinking over the phone call of the previous night and the unique problem that it poses for me. I knew within seconds of hanging up the telephone what my response would be, but it still troubles me. Some things are hard to confront, especially when they're personal. But I have no choice. I know what I must do and that gives me some comfort, but not enough. Not nearly enough.

While driving along the flat asphalt and concrete of the Connecticut highways, I keep my speed at an even sixty miles per hour, conscious of the eager state police who patrol these roads. Radar detectors are still illegal in this state and the police here seem to relish their role as adjuncts to the state's tax collection department. They have the best unmarked cars in the region, and I am in no mood to tempt them as I drive along.

Only once do I snap out of my reverie, and that's when two Harley-Davidson motorcycles rumble by, one on each side, the two men squat and burly in their low seats, long hair flapping in the breeze, goggles hiding their eyes, their denim vests and leather jackets looking too thin for this weather, their expressions saying they don't particularly care. The sight brings back some sharp memories: the wind in my face, the throb of the engine against my thighs, the almost Zen-like sense of traveling at high speed, just inches away from the asphalt and only seconds away from serious injury or death, and the certainty and comfort of what those motored bikes meant. Independence. Willing companions. Some sharp and tight actions. I almost sigh at the pleasurable memory. I have not ridden a motorcycle for years, and I doubt that I ever will again.

I'm busy with other things.

Somewhere in Massachusetts the morning and mid-morning coffee I have drunk has managed to percolate through my kidneys and is demanding to be released, and after some long minutes I see a sign that marks a rest area. As I pull into the short exit lane I see a smaller sign that in one line sums up the idiocy of highway engineering: No Sanitary Facilities. A rest area without a rest room. Why not.

There's a tractor-trailer parked at the far end of the lot, and the driver is out, slouched by the tires, examining something. Nearly a dozen cars have stopped and it seems odd to me that so many drivers have pulled over in this empty rest area. All this traffic, all these weary drivers, at this hour of this holiday morning?

I walk past the empty picnic tables, my leather boots crunching on the two or three inches of snow, when a man comes out from behind a tree. He's smoking a cigarette and he's shivering, and his knee-length leather coat is open, showing jeans and a white T-shirt. His blond hair is cut quite short, and he's to the point: "Looking for a date?"

The number of parked and empty cars now makes sense and I feel slightly foolish. I nod at the man and say, "Nope. Just looking for an empty tree," and keep on going. Some way to spend a holiday.

I find my empty tree and as I relieve myself against the pine trunk, I hear footsteps approach. I zip up and turn around and two younger men are there. One has a moustache and the other a beard, and both are wearing baseball caps with the bills pointed to the rear. Jeans, short black leather jackets, and sneakers mark their dress code. I smile and say, "No thanks, guys. I'm all set," as I walk away from the tree.

The one with the scraggly moustache laughs. "You don't understand, faggot. We're not all set."

Now they both have knives out, and the one with the beard says, "Turn over your wallet, 'fore we cut you where it counts."

I hold up my empty hands and say, "Jeez, no trouble, guys." I reach back and in a breath or two, my Beretta is in my hand, pointing at the two men. Their pasty-white faces deflate, like day-old balloons losing air, and I give them my best smile. They back up a few steps but I shake my head, and they stop, mouths still open in shock.

"Gee," I say. "Now I've changed my mind. I guess I'm not all set. Both knives, toss them behind you."

The knives are thrown behind them, making clattering noises as they strike tree branches and trunks before hitting the ground. The two young men turn again, arms held up, and the bearded one's hands are shaking.

"Very good," I say. I move the Beretta back and forth, scanning, so that one of the two is always covered. "Next I want those pants off and your wallets on the ground, and your jackets. No arguing."

The one with the moustache says, "You can't—"

I cock the hammer back on the Beretta. The noise sounds like a tree branch cracking from too much snow and ice.

"You don't listen well," I say. "No arguing."

The two slump to the ground and in a matter of moments the clothing is in a pile, and then they stand up again. Their arms go back up. One of the two—the one with the moustache—was not wearing any underwear and he is shriveled with cold and fear. Their legs are pasty white and quivering and I feel no pity whatsoever. I say, "Turn around, kneel down, and cross your ankles. Now."

They do as they're told, and I can see their bodies flinch as their bare skin strikes the snow and ice. I swoop down and pick up the clothing and say, "Move in the next fifteen minutes and you'll disappear, just like that."

I toss the clothing on the hood of my car and pull out a set of car keys and two wallets. From the wallets I take out a bundle of bills in various denominations, and I don't bother counting it. I just shove it into my pants pocket, throw everything into the car, and drive off.

After a mile I toss out the pants and jackets, and another mile after that, I toss out the car keys and wallets.

Too lenient, perhaps, but it is a holiday.

Ninety minutes later I pull over on a turn-off spot on Route 3, overlooking Boston Falls, the town which gave me the first years of my life. By now a light snow is falling and I check my watch. Ten minutes till one. Perfect timing.

Mother always has her Thanksgiving dinner at three p.m., and I'll be on time, with a couple of free hours for chitchat and time for some other things. I lean against the warm hood of the Mercedes and look at the mills and buildings of the town below me. *Self-portrait of the prodigal son returning,* I think, and what would make the picture perfect would be a cigarette in my hand, thin gray smoke curling above my head, as I think great thoughts.

But I haven't smoked in years, and the thoughts I think aren't great, they're just troubled.

I wipe some snow off the fender of the car. The snow is small and dry, and whispers away with no problem.

A few minutes later I pull up to 74 Wall Street, the place where I grew up, a street with homes lining it on either side. The house is a small Cape Cod which used to be a bright red and now suffers a covering of tan vinyl siding. In my mind's eye, this house is always red. It's surrounded by a chain-link fence that Father put up during the few years of retirement he enjoyed before dying ("All my life, all I wanted was a fence to keep those goddamn dogs in the neighborhood from pissing on my shrubs, and now I'm going to get it."). I hope he managed to enjoy it before coughing up his lungs at Manchester Memorial. Father never smoked a cigarette in his life, but the air in those mills never passed through a filter on its journey to his lungs. Parked in front of the house is the battered tan Subaru that belongs to my younger brother Owen and the blue Ford pickup truck that is owned by older brother Brad.

On Owen's Subaru there is a sticker on the rear windshield for the Society for the Protection of New Hampshire Forests, and on Brad's Ford is a sticker for the Manchester Police Benevolent Society. One's life philosophy, spelled out in paper and gummed labels. The rear windshield of my Mercedes is empty. They don't make stickers for what I do or believe in.

Getting out of the car, I barely make it through the front door of the house before I'm assaulted by sounds, smells, and a handful of small children in the living room. The smells are of turkey and fresh bread, and most of the sounds come from the children yelling, "Uncle Carl! Uncle Carl!" as they jump around me. There are three of them—all girls—and they belong to Brad and his wife Deena: Carey, age twelve; Corinne, age nine; and the youngest, Christine, age six. All have blond hair in various lengths and they grasp at me, saying the usual kid things of how much they miss me, what was I doing, would I be up here long, and of course, their favorite question:

"Uncle Carl, did you bring any presents?"

Brad is standing by the television set in the living room, a grimace pretending to be a smile marking his face. Deena looks up to him, troubled, and then manages a smile for me and that's all I need. I toss my car keys to Carey, the oldest.

"In the trunk," I say, "and there's also one for your cousin."

The kids stream outside and then my brother Owen comes in from the kitchen holding his baby son Todd, and he's followed by his wife Jan, and Mother. Owen tries to say something, but Mother barrels by and gives me the required hug, kiss, and why-don't-you-call-me-more look. Mother's looking fine, wearing an apron that one of us probably gave her as a birthday gift a decade or two ago, and her eyes are bright and alive behind her glasses. Most of her hair is gray and is pulled back in a bun, and she's wearing a floral print dress.

"My, you are looking sharp as always, Carl," she says admiringly, turning to see if Owen and Brad agree, and Owen smiles and Brad pretends to be watching something on television. Jan looks at me and winks, and I do nothing in return.

Mother goes back into the kitchen and I follow her and get a glass of water. When she isn't looking I reach up to a shelf and pull down a sugar bowl that contains her "mad money." I shove in the wad that I liberated earlier this day, and I return the bowl to the shelf, just in time to help stir the gravy.

As she works about the stove with me Owen comes in, still holding his son Todd, and Jan is with him. Owen sits down, looking up at me, holding the baby and its bottle, and it gurgles with what seems to be contentment. Owen's eyes are shiny behind his round, wire-rimmed glasses, and he says, "How are things in New York?"

"Cold," I say. "Loud. Dirty. The usual stuff."

Owen laughs and Jan joins in, but there's a different sound in her laugh. Owen is wearing a shapeless gray sweater and tan chinos, while Jan has on designer jeans and a buttoned light pink sweater that's about one button too many undone. Her brown hair is styled and shaped, and I can tell from her eyes that the drink in her hand isn't the first of the day.

"Maybe so," she says, "but at least it isn't boring, like some places people are forced to live."

Mother pretends to be busy about the stove and Owen is still smiling, though his eyes have faltered, as if he has remembered some old debt unpaid. I give Jan a sharp look and she just smiles and drinks, and I say to Owen, "How's the reporting?"

He shrugs, gently moving Todd back and forth. "The usual. Small-town stuff that doesn't get much coverage. But I've been thinking about starting a novel, nights when I get home from meetings. Something about small towns and small-town corruption."

Jan clicks her teeth against her glass. "Maybe your brother can help you. With some nasty ideas."

I finish off my water and walk past her. "Oh, I doubt that very much," I say, and I go into the living room, hearing the sound of Jan's laughter as I go.

The three girls have come back and the floor is a mess of shredded paper and broken boxes, as they ooh and aah over their gifts. There's a mix of clothing and dolls, the practical and the playful, because I know to the penny how much my older brother Brad makes each year and his budget is prohibitively tight.

His wife Deena is on the floor, playing with the girls, and she gives me a happy nod as I come in and sit down on the couch. She is a large woman and has on black stretch pants and a large blue sweater. I find that the more I get to know Deena, the more I like her. She comes from a farm family and makes no bones about having dropped out of high school at age sixteen. Though she's devoted utterly and totally to my brother, she also has a sharp rural way of looking at things, and though I'm sure Brad has told her many awful stories about me, she has also begun to trust her own feelings. I think she likes me, though I know she would never admit that to Brad.

Brad is sitting in an easy chair across the way, intent on looking at one of the Thanksgiving Day parades. He's wearing sensible black shoes, gray slacks, and an orange sweater, and pinned to one side is a turkey button, probably given to him by one of his daughters. Brad has a thin moustache and his black hair is slicked back, for he started losing it at age sixteen. He looks all right, though there's a roll of fat beginning to swell about his belly.

"How's it going, Brad?" I ask, sending out the first peace feeler.

"Oh, not bad," he says, eyes not leaving the screen.

"Detective work all right? Got any interesting cases you're working on?"

"Unh hunh," and he moves a glass of what looks like milk from one hand to the other.

"Who do you think will win the afternoon game?" I try again.

He shrugs. "Whoever has the best team, I imagine."

Well. Deena looks up again, troubled, and I just give her a quiet nod, saying with my look that everything's all right, and then I get up from the couch and go outside and get my winter coats and overnight bag and bring them back inside. I drop them off upstairs in the tiny room that used to be my bedroom so many years and memories ago, and then I look into a mirror over a battered bureau and say, "Time to get to work," and that makes me laugh. For the first time in a long time I'm working gratis.

I go downstairs to the basement, switching on the overhead fluorescents, which *click-click-hum* into life. Father's old workbench is in one corner, and dumped near the workbench is a pile of firewood for the living room fireplace. The rest of the basement is taken up with boxes, old bicycles, and a washer and dryer. The basement floor is concrete and relatively clean. I go upstairs fast, taking two steps at a time. Brad is in the living room, with his three girls, trying to show some enthusiasm for the gifts I brought. I call out to him and he looks up.

"Yeah?" he says.

"C'mere," I say, excitement tingeing my voice. "You won't believe what I found."

He pauses for a moment, as if debating with himself whether he should ever trust his younger brother, and I think his cop curiosity wins out, for he says, " 'Scuse me," to his daughters and ambles over.

"What's going on?" he says in that flat voice I think cops learn at their service academy.

"Downstairs," I say. "I was poking around and behind Father's workbench there's an old shoebox. Brad, it looks like your baseball card collection, the one Mother thought she tossed away."

For the first time I get a reaction out of Brad and a grin pops into life. "Are you sure?"

"Sure looks like it to me. C'mon down and take a look."

Brad brushes by me and thunders downstairs on the plain wooden steps, and I follow close behind, saying, "You've got to stretch across the table and really take a close look, Brad, but I think it's them."

He says, "My God, it's been almost twenty years since I've seen them. Think of how much money they could be worth . . . "

In front of the workbench Brad leans over, casting his head back and forth, his orange sweater rising up, treating me to a glimpse of his bare back and the top of his hairy buttocks, and he says, "Carl, I don't see—"

And with that I pick up a piece of firewood and pound it into the back of his skull.

Brad makes a coughing sound and falls on top of the workbench and I kick away his legs and he swears at me and in a minute or two of tangled struggle, he ends up on his back. I straddle his chest, my knees digging into his upper arms, a forearm pressed tight against his throat, and he gurgles as I slap his face with my free hand.

"Do I have your attention, older brother?"

He curses some more and struggles, and I press in again with my forearm and replay the slapping. I'm thankful that no one from upstairs has heard us. I say, "Older brother, I'm younger, faster, and stronger, and we need to talk; if you'll stop thrashing around, we'll get somewhere."

Another series of curses, but then he starts gurgling louder and nods, and I ease up on the forearm and say, "Just how stupid do you have to be before you stop breathing, Brad?"

"What the hell are you doing, you maniac?" he demands, his voice a loud whisper. "I'm gonna have you arrested for assault, you no-good—"

I lean back with the forearm and he gurgles some more and I say, "Listen once, and listen well, older brother. I got a phone call last night from an old friend saying my police-detective brother is now in the pocket of one Bill Sutler. You mind telling me how the hell that happened?"

His eyes bug out and I pull back my forearm and he says, "I don't know what the hell you're talking about, you lowlife biker."

Two more slaps to the face. "First, I'm no biker and you know it. Second, I'm talking about Bill Sutler, who handles the numbers and other illegal adventures for this part of this lovely state. I'm talking about an old friend I can trust with my life telling me that you now belong to this charming gentleman. Now. Let's stop dancing and start talking, shall we?"

Brad's eyes are piggish and his face is red, his slick black hair now a tangle, and I'm preparing for another struggle or another series of denials, and then it's like a dam that has been ruptured, a wall that has been breached, for I feel his body loosen underneath me, and he turns his face. "Shit," he whispers.

"Gambling?" I ask.

He just nods. "How much?" I ask again.

"Ten K," he says. "It's the vig that's killing me, Carl, week after week, and now, well, now he wants more than just money."

"Of course," I say, leaning back some. "Information. Tip-offs. Leads on some investigations involving him and his crew."

Brad looks up and starts talking and I slap him again, harder, and I lean back into him and say in my most vicious tone, "Where in hell have you been storing your brains these past months, older brother? Do you have even the vaguest idea of what you've gotten yourself into? Do you think a creature like Bill Sutler is going to let you go after a couple of months? Of course not, and if he ever gets arrested by the state or the feds, he's going to toss you up for a deal so fast you'll think the world is spinning backwards."

He tries to talk but I keep plowing on. "Then let's take it from there, after you get turned over. Upstairs is a woman who loves you so much she'd probably go after this Sutler guy with her bare hands if she could, and you have three daughters who think you're the best daddy in the Western Hemisphere. Not to mention a woman who thinks you're the good son, the successful one, and a younger brother who wishes he could be half the man you pretend you are. Think of how they'll all do, how they'll live, when they see you taken away to the state prison in orange overalls."

By now Brad is silently weeping, the tears rolling down his quivering cheeks, and I feel neither disgust nor pity. It's what I expected, what I planned for, and I say, "Then think about what prison will be like, you, a cop, side by side with some rough characters who would leap at a chance to introduce you to some hard loving. Do I have your attention now, older brother? Do I?"

He's weeping so much that he can only nod, and then I get off his chest and stand up and he rolls over, in a fetal position, whispering faint obscenities, over and over again, and I don't mind since they're not aimed at me.

"Where does this guy Sutler live?" I ask.

"Purmort," he says.

"Get up," I say. "I'm going to pay him a visit, and you're going to help."

Brad sits up, snuffling, and leans back against the wooden workbench. "You're going to see him? Now? An hour before Thanksgiving dinner? You're crazy, even for a biker."

I shrug, knowing that I will be washing my hands momentarily. They look clean, but right now they feel quite soiled. "He'll talk to me, and you're going to back me up, because I'm saving your sorry ass this afternoon."

Brad looks suspicious. "What does that mean?"

"You'll find out, soon enough."

Before Brad can say anything, the door upstairs opens up and Deena calls down, "Hey, you guys are missing the parade."

I look at Brad and he's rubbing at his throat. I reply to Deena, "So we are, so we are."

Fifteen minutes later I pull into Founder's Park, near the Bellamy River, in an isolated section of town. Of course it's deserted on this special day and I point out an empty park bench, near two snow-covered picnic tables. "Go sit there and contemplate your sorry life."

"What?"

"I said, get out there and contemplate your sorry life. I'm going to talk to this Sutler character alone."

"But—"

"I'm getting you out of trouble today, older brother, and all I ask from you is one thing. That you become my alibi. Anything comes up later today or next week that has to do with me, you're going to swear as a gentleman and a police officer that the two of us were just driving around at this time of the day, looking at the town and having some fond recollections before turkey dinner. Understand?"

Brad looks stubborn for a moment and says, "It's cold out there."

I reach behind me and pull out the thermos bottle that Raphael had packed for me, so many hours and places ago. "Here. I freshened it up at the house a while ago, before we left. Go out there and sit and I'll be back."

That same stubborn look. "Why are you doing this for me?"

I lean over him and open the door. "Not for you. For the family. Get out, will you? I don't want to be late."

At last he steps out and walks over to the park bench, the thermos bottle in his humiliated hands, and he sits down and stares out at the frozen river. He doesn't look my way as I pull out and head to Purmort.

I've parked the Mercedes on a dirt road that leads into an abandoned gravel pit, and I have a long wool winter coat on over my cardigan sweater. The air is still and some of the old trees still have coverings of snow looking like plastic casts along the branches. There's a faint maze of animal tracks in the snow, and I recognize the prints of a rabbit and a squirrel. I'm leaning against the front hood of the Mercedes as a black Ford Bronco ambles up the dirt path. It parks in front of my car and I feel a quick tinge of unease: I don't like having my escape routes blocked, and then the unease grows as two men get out of the Bronco. I had only been expecting one.

The man on the right moves a bit faster than his companion and I figure that he's Bill Sutler. My guess is correct, and it is he who begins to chatter at me.

"Let me start off by saying I don't like you already for two reasons," he says in a gravelly tone that's either come from throat surgery or too many cigarettes at an early age. He's just a few inches shorter than me, and though his black hair is balding, he has a long strip at the back tied in a ponytail. Fairly fancy for this part of the state. His face is slightly pockmarked with old acne scars, and he has on a bright blue ski jacket with the obligatory tattered ski passes hanging from the zipper. Jeans and dull orange construction boots finish off his ensemble.

"Why's that?" I say, arms and legs crossed, still leaning against the warm hood of my Mercedes, my boots in the snow cover.

"Because you pulled me out of my house on Thanksgiving, and because of your license plates," he says, pointing to the front of my Mercedes, talking fast, his entire face seemingly squinting at me. "You're from New York, and I hate guys from New York who think they can breeze in here and throw their weight around. You're in my woods now, guy, and I don't care what games you've played back on your crappy island. We do things different up here."

His companion has stepped away from the passenger's side of the Bronco and is keeping watch on me. He seems a bit younger but he's considerably more bulky, with a tangle of curly hair and a thick beard. He's wearing an army fatigue coat and the same jeans/boot combination that Sutler is sporting. I note that the right pocket of his coat is sagging some, from the weight of something inside.

I nod over to the second man. "That your muscle, along to keep things quiet?"

Sutler turns his head for a moment. "That there's Kelly, and he's here because I want him here. I tell him to leave, he'll leave. I tell him to break every finger on your hands, he'd do that, too. So let's leave him out of things right now. Talk. You got me here, what do you want?"

I rub at my chin. "I want something that you have. I want

Brad Curtis's *cojones,* and I understand you have them in your pocket."

Sutler smirks. "That I do. What's your offer?"

This just might be easy. "In twenty-four hours, I settle his gambling debt," I say. "I also put in a word to a couple of connected guys, and some extra business gets tossed your way. You get your money, you get some business, and I get what I want. You also never have any contact or dealings with him again, any time in the future."

"You're a relation, right?"

I nod. "His brother."

"Younger or older?"

"Younger."

Sutler smirks again, and I decide I don't like the look. "Isn't that sweet. Well, look at this, younger brother. The answer is no."

I cock my head. "Is that a real no, or do you want a counter offer? If it's a counter offer, mention something. I'm sure I can be reasonable."

He laughs and rocks back on his heels a bit and says, "Little one, this isn't a negotiation. The answer is no."

"Why?"

That stops him for a moment, and there's a furtive gesture from his left hand, and Kelly steps a bit closer. "Because I already told you," he says. "I don't like you New York guys, and I don't trust you. Sure, you'd probably pay off the money, but everything else you say is probably crap. You think I'm stupid? Well, I think you're stupid, and here's why. I got something good in that nitwit detective, and you and your New York friends aren't going to take it away. I got him and my work here on my own, and I don't need your help. Understand?"

"Are you sure?"

Another laugh. "You think I'm giving up a detective on the largest police force in this state for you? The stuff he can feed me is pure gold, little one, and it's gonna set me for life. There's nothing you have that can match that. Nothing."

He gestures again. "And I'm tired of you, and I'm tired of this crap. I'm going back home."

"Me too," I say, and I slide my hand into the cardigan, pull out my Beretta, and blow away Kelly's left knee.

Kelly is on the ground, howling, and the echo of the shot is still bouncing about the hills as I slam the Beretta into the side of Sutler's head. He falls, and I stride over to Kelly. Amid his thrashings on the now-bloody snow, I grab a .357 revolver from his coat and toss it into the woods. In a matter of heartbeats I'm back to Sutler, who's on the ground, fumbling to get into his ski jacket. I kick him solidly in the crotch. He yelps and then I'm on him, the barrel of the Beretta jamming into his lips until he gags and has a couple of inches of the oily metal in his mouth. His eyes are very wide and there's a splotch of blood on his left cheek. I take a series of deep breaths, knowing that I want my voice cool and calm.

"About sixty seconds ago I was interested in negotiating with you, but now I've lost interest. Do you understand? If you do, nod your head, but nod it real slow. It's cold and my fingers are beginning to get numb."

His eyes are tearing and he nods, just like I said. "Very good," I say, trying to place a soothing tone in my voice. "I came here in a good mood, in a mood to make a deal that could help us both, and all you've done since we've met is insult me. Do you think I got up early this morning and drove half the day so a creature like you can toss insults my way? Do you?"

Though I didn't explain to him the procedure for shaking

his head, Sutler shows some initiative and gently shakes it. Kelly, some yards away, is still groaning and occasionally crying. I ignore him because I want to, and I think Sutler is ignoring him because he has to.

"Now," I continue. "If you had some random brain cells in that sponge between your ears, I think you would have figured out that because this matter involves my brother, I might have a personal interest in what was going on. But you were too stupid to realize that, correct?"

Another nod of the head, and saliva and blood is beginning to drip down the barrel of the Beretta. "So instead of accepting a very generous offer, you said no and insulted me. So you left me no choice. I had to show you how serious I was, and I had to make an impression."

I gesture over to the sobbing hulk of his companion. "Take a look at Kelly if you can. I don't know the man, I have nothing against him, and if the two of us had met under different circumstances, we might have become friends."

Well, I doubt that, but I keep my doubts to myself. I am making a point. "But I had to make an example," I continue, "and in doing so, I've just crippled Kelly for life. Do you understand that? His knee is shattered and he'll never walk well again for the next thirty or forty years of his life because of your ill manners and stubbornness. Now. You having rejected my offer, here's my counteroffer. Are you now interested?"

Another nod, a bit more forceful. "Good. Here it is. You forget the gambling debt. You forget you ever knew my brother, and you take poor Kelly here to a hospital and tell them that he was shot in a hunting accident or something. I don't care. And if you ever bother my brother or his family, any time in the future, I'll come back."

I poke the Beretta in another centimeter or two, and Sutler

groans. "Then I'll find out who counts most in your life—your mother, your wife, your child, for all I know—and I'll do the same thing to them that I did to Kelly. Oh, I could make it permanent, but a year or two after the funeral, you usually get on with life. Not with this treatment. The person suffers in your presence, for decades to come, because of you. Now. Is the deal complete?"

Sutler closes his teary eyes and nods, and I get up, wiping the Beretta's barrel on his ski jacket. Sutler is grimacing and the crotch of his pants is wet and steaming in the cold. Kelly is curled up on his side, weeping, his left leg a bloody mess, and I take a step back and gently prod Sutler with my foot.

"Move your Bronco, will you?" I ask politely.

My brother's face is a mix of anger and hope as he climbs back into my Mercedes, rubbing his hands from the cold. His face and ears are quite red.

"Well?" he asks.

"Piece of cake," I say, and I drive back to the house.

Dinner is long and wonderful, and I have a sharp appetite and eat well, sitting at the far end of the table. My nieces good-naturedly fight over the supposed honor of sitting next to me, which makes Mother and Deena laugh, and even Brad attempts a smile or two. I stuff myself and we regale each other with stories of holidays and Christmases and Thanksgivings past, and Owen bounces Todd on his knee as Jan smiles to herself and sips from one glass of wine and then another.

I feel good belonging here with them. Though I know that none of them quite knows who I am or what I do, it's still a comfortable feeling. It's like nothing else I experience, ever, and I cherish it.

★ ★ ★ ★ ★

Later, I take a nap in my old bedroom, and feeling greasy from the day's exertions and the long meal, I take a quick shower, remembering a lot of days and weeks and years gone past as I climb into the tiny stall. It seems fairly humorous that I am in this house taking a weak and lukewarm shower after having remembered this creaky bathroom earlier this morning, back at my Manhattan home. That explains why I am smiling when I go back into my old bedroom, threadbare light green towel wrapped around my waist, and I find Jan there, waiting for me, my brother Owen's wife.

Her eyes are aglitter and her words are low and soft, but there's a hesitation there, as if she realizes she has been drinking for most of the day and she has to be careful in choosing each noun and verb. She's standing by an old bureau, jean-encased hip leaning up against the wood, and she has something in her hands.

"Look at this, will you," she says. "Found it up here while I was waiting for you."

I step closer and I can smell the alcohol on her breath, and I also smell something a bit earthier. I try not to sigh, seeing the eager expression on her face. I take her offering and turn it over. It's an old color photograph, and it shows a heavyset man with a beard and long hair in a ponytail sitting astride a black Harley-Davidson motorcycle. He's wearing the obligatory jeans and leather vest. His arms are tattooed. The photo is easily a decade old, and in those years the chemicals on the print have faded and mutated, so that there's an eerie yellow glow about everything, as if the photo were taken at a time when volcanic ash was drifting through the air.

I look closely at the photo and then hand it back to my sister-in-law. About the only thing I recognize about the person is the eyes, for it's the only thing about me that I've not changed since that picture was taken.

"That's really you, isn't it?" she asks, that eager tone in her voice still there. With her in my old room, everything seems crowded. There's a tiny closet, the bureau, a night table, and lumpy bed with thin blankets and sheets. A window about the size of a pie plate looks out to the pale green vinyl siding of the house next door.

"Yes, that's me," I say. "Back when I was younger and dumber."

She licks her lips. "Asking questions about you of Owen is a waste of time, and your mother and Brad aren't much help either. You were a biker, right?"

I nod. "That's right."

"What was it like, Carl?" she asks, moving a few inches closer to me. I know I should feel embarrassed, standing in my old bedroom with my sister-in-law, just wearing a towel, but I'm not sure what I feel. I just know it's not embarrassment. So instead of debating the point, I answer her question.

"It was like moving to a different country and staying at home, all at the same time," I say. "There was an expression, something about being free and being a citizen. Being free meant the bike and your friends and whatever money you had for gas and food, and the time to travel anywhere you wanted, any time, with no one to stop you, feeling the wind in your hair and face. Being a citizen meant death, staying at home, paying taxes, and working a forty-hour week. That's what it was like."

She gives me a sharp-toothed smile. "You almost make it sound like a Boy Scout troop. Way your older brother talks, I figure you've been in trouble."

I shrug. "Comes with the territory. It's something you get used to. Being free means you run into a lot of different people, and sometimes their tempers are short and their memories are long. Sometimes you do some work for some money that wouldn't look good on a job application form."

"So that explains the scars?" she asks.

"Yeah, I guess it does."

"So why did you change? What happened? From the picture, I can tell you've had your tattoos taken off."

I look around and see that my clothes are still on the bed where I left them. "I got tired of having my life depend on other people. Thing is, you run with a group, the group can sometimes pull you down. What the group accomplishes can come back at night and break your windows, or gnaw on your leg. And I didn't want to become a citizen. So I chose a bit of each world and made my own, and along the way I changed my look."

"And what do you do now? Everyone says consulting work, but they always have an uncomfortable look on their face when they mention that, like they have gas or something. So what's your job?"

I pause and say, "Systems engineer."

Her eyes blink in amusement. "A what?"

"Systems engineer. Sometimes a system needs an outside pressure or force to make a necessary change or adjustment. That's what I do. I'm an independent contractor."

"Sounds very exciting," she says, arching an eyebrow this time. "You should talk some to your younger brother. Maybe pass some of that excitement along. Or maybe you're the brother who got it all in this family."

I now feel an aching sorrow for Owen, and I try not to think of what their pillow talk must be like at night. "Guess you have to work with what you've got."

"Unh-hunh," she says. "Look, you must be getting cold. Are you going to get dressed, or what?"

I decide she wants a show, or wants something specific to

happen, so I say, "Or what, I suppose." I turn to the bed and drop the towel and get dressed, and I hear a hush of breath coming from her. After the underwear, pants, and boots, I turn, buttoning my shirt, and she's even closer and I reach to her and she comes forward, lips wet, and then I strike out and put a hand around her throat. And I squeeze.

"Jan," I say, stepping forward and looking into her eyes, "you and I are about to come to an agreement, do you understand?"

"What are you doing, you—" and I squeeze again, and she makes a tiny yelping sound, and her nostrils begin to flare as she tries to breathe harder. She starts to flail with her hands and I grab one hand and press her against the bureau. It shakes and she tries to kick, but I'm pushing at her at an uncomfortable angle, and she can't move.

"This won't take long, but I ask that you don't yell. You try to yell and I'll squeeze hard enough to make you black out. Do you understand? Try blinking your eyes."

She blinks, tears forming in her eyes. My mind plays with a few words and then I say, "Owen and my family mean everything to me. Everything. And right now, by accident of marriage and the fact of my brother's love, you're part of this family. But not totally. My mother and Owen and even Brad come before you. You're not equal in my eyes, do you understand?"

She moves her head a bit, and I'm conscious that I might have to take another shower when I'm finished. "So that's where I'm coming from when I tell you this: I don't care if you love my brother or hate my brother, but I do demand this. That you show him respect. He deserves that. Stay with him or leave him tonight, I don't care. But don't toss yourself to those random men that manage to cross your path, especially ones related to him. If you can't stand being with him, leave, but do it with dignity. Show him respect or I'll hurt you, Jan."

"You're hurting me now," she whispers.

"No, I'm not," I explain. "I'm not hurting you. I'm getting your attention. In an hour you'll be just fine, but in a hundred years you're always going to remember this conversation in this dingy bedroom. Am I right?"

She nods and I say, "So we've reached an understanding. Agreed?"

Another nod and I let her go and back away, and Jan rubs at her throat and coughs. Then she whispers a dark series of curses and leaves, slamming the door behind her, and what scares me is that she isn't crying, not one tear, not one sign of regret or fear.

I finish getting dressed, trying not to think of Owen.

Despite a lumpy bed and too-silent surroundings of Boston Falls, I sleep fairly well that night, with none of those disturbing dreams of loud words and sharp actions that sometimes bring me awake. I get up with the sun and slowly walk through the living room to the kitchen. Sprawled across the carpeted floor in sleeping bags are my three nieces—Carey, Corinne, and Christine—and their shy innocence and the peacefulness of their slight breathing touches something inside of me that I wasn't sure even existed anymore.

Mother is in the kitchen and I give her a brief hug and grab a cup of coffee. I try not to grimace as I sip the brew; Mother, God bless her, has never made a decent cup of coffee in her life. I've been dressed since getting up and Mother is wearing a faded blue bathrobe, and as she stirs a half-dozen eggs in a mixing bowl she looks over at me through her thick glasses and says, "I'm not that dumb, you know."

I gamely try another sip of coffee. "I've always known that, ever since you found my collection of girlie magazines when I was in high school."

"Bah," she says, stirring the whisk harder. "I knew you had those for a while, and I knew boys always get curious at that age. I didn't mind much until your younger brother Owen was snooping around. Then I couldn't allow it. He was too young."

She throws in a bit of grated cheese and goes back to the bowl and says, "Are you all right, Carl?"

"Just fine."

"I wonder," she says. "Yesterday you were roaming around here like a panther at the zoo, and then you and Brad go off for a mysterious trip. You said it was just a friendly trip, but the two of you haven't been friends for years. You do something bad out there?"

I think about Kelly with the shattered leg and Bill Sutler with his equally ruined day, and I say, "Yeah, I suppose so."

Her voice is sharp. "Was it for Brad?"

Even Mother probably can see the surprise on my face, so I say, "Yes, it was for Brad."

"You hurt someone?"

I nod. "But he deserved it, Mom."

Then she puts down her utensils and wipes her hands on her apron and says, "That's what you do for a living, isn't it, Carl? You hurt people."

Right then I wish the coffee tasted better, for I could take a sip and gain a few seconds for a response, but Mother is looking right through me and I say, "You're absolutely right."

She sighs. "But yesterday was for Brad. And the money you send me, and the gifts for your nieces, and everything else, all comes from your job. Hurting people."

"That's right."

Mother goes back to the eggs, starts whisking again with the wire beater, and says, "I've known that for a very long time, ever since you claimed you quit being a biker. I just

knew you went on to something different, something probably even worse, though you certainly dressed better and
looked clean."

She looks over again. "Thank you for the truth, Carl. And
I'll never ask you again, you can believe that. Just tell me that
what you do is right, and that you're happy."

So I tell her what she wants to hear, and she gives me another hug, and then there's some noise as the kids get up.

And then after breakfast it's time to go, and though Jan
hangs back and says nothing, the kids are all over me, as is
Mother, and even Deena—Brad's wife—gives me a peck on
the cheek. Owen shakes my hand and I tell him to call me,
anytime, making sure that Jan has heard me. And then there's
the surprise, as Brad shakes my hand for the first time in a
very long year or five.

"Thanks," he says. "And, um, well, come by sometime.
The girls do miss you."

With that one sentence playing in my mind, I drive for
over an hour, not bothering with the music on my CD player,
for I'm hearing louder music in my head.

Later that night I'm in my large sunken tub, a small metal
pitcher of vodka martinis on the marble floor. Sarah is in the
tub with me, suds up to her lovely and full chest, and her hair
is drawn up around her head, making her look like a Gibson
Girl from the turn of the century. I talk for some minutes and
she laughs a few times and then reaches out with a wet and
soapy foot and caresses my side. Like myself, she's holding a
glass full of ice cubes and clear liquid.

"Only a guy like you, Carl, could travel hours to your family's home on a holiday weekend and bring your work with
you," she says.

I sink a bit in the tub, feeling the hot water relax my back muscles. It had snowed some on the way back, and I'm still a bit tense from the drive.

"It wasn't work," I say. "It was a favor, a family thing."

"Mmmm," she says, sipping from her glass. "So that makes it all right?"

I shrug. "It just makes it, I guess."

"A worthwhile trip, then?"

"Very," I say, drinking from my own glass, enjoying the slightly oily bite of the drink. She sighs again and says, "You never really answered me, you know."

I close my eyes and say, "I didn't know I owed you an answer."

She nudges me with her foot. "Brute. From Thursday morning. When I asked you why you went there. And all you could say was family. Is that it, Carl? Truly?"

I know the true answer, which is that the little group of people in that tiny town are the only thing I have that is not bought or paid for in blood, and that keeping that little tie alive and well is important, very important to me. For if that tie were broken, then whatever passes for a human being in me would shrivel up and rot away, and I could not allow that. That is the truth, but I don't feel like debating philosophy tonight.

So I say, "Haven't you heard the expression?"

"What's that?"

I raise my drink to her in a toast. "Even the bad can do good."

Sarah makes a face and tosses the drink's contents at me, and then water starts slopping over onto the floor, and the lovely evening gets even lovelier, and there's no more talk of family and obligations, which is just fine.

This story proves, I suppose, that even if a story is first rejected, if you like it and it has merit, it will eventually find a home. This story was turned down by the standard mystery magazines, and went straight into a file folder in my office. Then, one day the Sunday magazine of the Boston Herald newspaper called, looking for a mystery story. This went out in the mail and a few days later, the editor bought it. The gritty urban environment in this story, fortunately, no longer exists in most American cities.

Thieves

The heavy and unmarked blue car was parked at the street corner, next to a burned-out drugstore. The "D" and "R" were the only letters not blackened on the boarded-up building. It was dusk and the shattered streetlights up and down the street made no sound. The bulletproof car windows were slightly open, letting in a breeze that smelled of old smoke and wet garbage. Two men the size of hockey players sat in the front of the car and Miller sat in the rear, listening to them talk. The breeze made scraps of cardboard, newspaper and fast food wrappers skitter along the cracked asphalt.

"My cousin's doing all right," Jacob said, his arms draped over the steering wheel. "Left the county prison job last year, did I tell you that? He's at one of those detention camps, up at the National Forest. Better food and you're outdoors a lot."

His companion Samuel laughed ruefully. "Yeah. Nice work, if you can get it."

Miller shifted in the seat, feeling oppressed and uncomfortable, sweat trickling down his skin. His suit was too tight because of the adjustable body armor he was wearing around his arms, legs and torso. He had no weapons. The weapons were at the front of the car. Jacob and Samuel wore blue nylon windbreakers and khaki slacks over their personal body armor, and as they talked their eyes kept moving around, searching and evaluating. Between them, slung underneath the dashboard, a police radio crackled and hissed out messages.

There were tenement buildings all up and down the streets. Most of the windows in the buildings were still dark. On the left, across the street, was a vacant lot with three shattered cars and mounds of brick and rubble. Two darkened tenement buildings stood at the far end. Miller kept looking over to the lot. There was movement there, of people floating in and out of the two buildings.

At Miller's side, on the smooth and worn upholstery, was a thick file. In one corner a typewritten label said Henry Williams. The file's cover was smudged and dirty, with a brown half-ring in the middle from being used as a coaster. Henry Williams. Their target for the night. And he knew the file well.

In the distance: *pop-pop. Pop-pop.*

In the front seat, both heads turned to the sound.

"Handgun?" Jacob asked.

"Handgun," Samuel agreed. "You get that light, airy sound. Sounds like a nine millimeter."

Neither of them looked to the rear seat. Miller knew why. The field boys hated having a suit ride along. But on special assignments like tonight, it was required. Procedures.

"Getting hungry," Jacob said. Samuel turned in the seat, the seat fabric squeaking, and he said, "This Williams boy? What time you expect him?"

Miller said, "Past surveillances say he usually goes out

about now. Any minute should do it."

Samuel turned back and said, "Well, we'll eat afterwards. I know a nice drive-through, couple of blocks away. Beats eating at the old precinct house. You like the precinct house, Miller? You got a nice office there?"

Jacob laughed and Miller smiled, saying, "It's on the third floor. A cubicle with a phone that doesn't work half the time, and a barred window that looks down on the parking lot. Not exactly what I've been used to."

"My man," Miller said, looking at Jacob with a wide grin. "The man's got a cubicle. Hoo-boy. He must be very high up. You and me and everybody else are in that dog pound that used to be a squad room."

The two of them laughed and Miller wondered again for a hundredth time what he was doing out here, and he looked again at the bulky forms of Jacob and Samuel. He hated depending on them for his safety but he was out of his element on the streets. There was no denying that. He was one for navigating some treacherous waters in his career, in stroking the right egos at the right time and knowing when to cut someone down, but that was nothing compared to the streets. At his old job, losing a good one meant going home and having a stiff drink and vowing to do better tomorrow. Out here, losing one—good or bad—could mean a trip to the crowded and bleeding swamp that passed as a hospital nowadays in this part of the city.

And during many sleepless nights the past few months, he had wondered about this assignment. A lot of opportunity, he was told at the beginning, a lot of opportunity was here for his taking, and he nodded again as he thought of that. Yeah, a lot of opportunity. A lot of opportunity to screw up, and a very small opportunity to make a difference.

And the eyes, he thought, shivering even though he was

sweaty from the body armor. The blank eyes of those he saw down here, every day. It was like nothing he had ever seen before.

"You know," Jacob said, starting to tap a rhythm on a steering wheel, "I read somewhere that in Japan, they've taken over one of those islands they got, you know, the ones the volcanoes make?"

"Yeah?"

"Yeah," he said. "Then they took all the cons, the ones with drug offenses above a certain level, and they dumped 'em there, with some food and water and tools and stuff, and that's it. They're on their own. No guards, no wardens, nothing. There's a couple of Coast Guard cutters that roam around the island and shoot at whoever tries to get off."

Samuel yawned and leaned his head against a hand. "That so? The article say what they're doin' in Germany?"

"Nope." Jacob swiveled in his seat. "You know, Miller? What are they doing in Germany?"

He reached down and touched Henry Williams' file. "Pollution brigades. Chain gangs that are sent into cities and towns in the old East Germany. They're cleaning up about fifty years worth of pollution. They work with some really rugged stuff, until the gangs get cranked out. Then they bring in some new ones and put them to work. That's what they're doing. Very efficient."

"Yeah," Jacob said. "Good Germans and all that."

There was a sound of sirens and two city police cruisers roared by, bumper-to-bumper, strobe-bars flashing. The cruisers were dented and one car had a burned-out headlight. Each cruiser had two policemen in the front seat.

"Used to be," Jacob said, arms still over the steering wheel, still looking around, "that a cop and a cruiser would be sent out. Then things got so bad that they put two cops in a cruiser. Now we're up to having two cruisers assigned to each other. Some progress. What's next?"

Samuel grunted and sat lower in his seat, his arms folded together. "Air support. Or artillery, though Jesus, this town's pretty shot up as it is."

Miller looked over again at the blasted-out lot across the street, and saw that some of the figures were carrying something in their hands. They were moving cautiously about the piles of debris, heading to the two tenement buildings. Miller said, "Check out the movement over there, in the lot."

Jacob and Samuel leaned over and looked out the driver's side window. Jacob said, "Looks like about six or seven, heading to the buildings. Probably a couple of smokehouses there."

Samuel held a tiny pair of binoculars up to his eyes. "They are carrying some serious heat, my friends."

"AKs?" Miller asked.

Samuel whistled. "Jesus, everybody down here's got an AK, but these boy-os got AKS-74s. Top of the line. And some of them have some RPG-7s—shoulder-held rocket launchers."

"Well, I—"

Gunfire suddenly erupted from the lot and Jacob rolled up the bulletproof window, and Miller watched tracers leap out from behind the rubble mounds and tattoo against the two buildings. From some of the darkened windows little flashes of light winked back, as the gunfight intensified.

Jacob made a motion to the police radio and Miller said, "Hold it."

"Hunh?" He turned his head. "I know it's not our fight, but at least we could call it in anonymously, get some units down here."

The hard *slap-slap* of the automatic weapons echoed

across the streets. Miller felt his chest tighten and thought, *an MBA from one of the best colleges in the country, and I'm here, doing this?*

"No," he said. "That's not our worry. Our worry tonight is Henry Williams. We call down some units now, we might scare him off. And we might lose him, and that would not be very nice at all. Leave the radio alone, Jacob. What's going on over there is not our concern."

He swore and drew his hand back from the console and Samuel, binoculars still at his face, said, "Relax, Jacob. Big city like this, you gotta expect to take a couple of hits."

"I know," Jacob said, "but it seems so—"

There was a low *whoosh* and another, and the dull thumps of explosions. Some of the gunfire from the two buildings began to die away. *God's always on the side with the heaviest artillery,* Miller thought. Someone had taught him that once, at a time when he was at school and the heaviest drug was beer and maybe some grass.

"RPG?" Jacob asked.

"Oh, most definitely," Samuel said, lowering his binoculars. "You know, this could be a neighborhood vigilante group. Doesn't have to be rival gangs. People who don't want smoke houses in their neighborhood."

"Yeah, right." Jacob shook his head. The gunfire had dropped away to random shots. "Remember when crack houses used to be so bad? Man, they're nothing compared to the smoke houses. Lock you and five or six others in a room and toss in the lit punk, and you rent the room by the hour. Remember that case, on the Lower East Side, when they found those six kids? They had been smoked out so much they had starved to death. Hadn't even bothered to move. And the guy that ran the smoke house, he said, 'So what? They were paid up for a week. I don't care what they did.' "

"Real cheerful attitude," Samuel said.

"You know—hey, Miller, look ahead. Is this your Henry?"

Miller felt his mouth dry out and he leaned forward, looking between the two men. Without having to look at the file, he recognized the young man walking across the street, scurrying away from the sounds of the gunfire, carrying a paper sack under his arm. He was dressed in jeans, sneakers, and a dark blue dungaree jacket. Henry Williams. Sixteen years old and my friend, how much you have accomplished in your short life.

"That's him," Miller said, hoping his voice didn't quaver. "Let's do it."

"You got it," Jacob said, starting the car's engine.

Samuel leaned back against his seat and rubbed his hands together. "Man, it's good to be moving. Sitting still equals being a target in this neighborhood."

As the car pulled out Miller turned one more time and saw that the two tenement buildings were burning, and every time someone ran from the blaze, a gunshot would pound out.

Henry Williams, he thought. *Henry Williams*.

It was easy, so very easy.

Jacob drove up the street and they passed Henry Williams, who was walking fast, the bag clenched under his arm. Jacob made a left turn and then circled around, and headed back to the youth. Miller's mouth was still very dry and Samuel looked over and winked and said, "Relax, Miller. We've done this a hundred times, and haven't lost anyone yet."

"We lost that girl last August," Jacob said, his voice flat, both hands on the steering wheel.

Samuel hunched forward and pulled out his weapon, a black automatic pistol that seemed almost as long as his arm. "Not our fault. She had been knifed before our pickup. Least we got her to a clean hospital to die in. That's better than the streets. Here we go."

The car braked suddenly to a stop and the doors flew open, as Jacob slammed the car into park. Henry Williams looked up, his eyes wide with fear, and he turned to run but Samuel was upon him, impossible, Samuel being so big, but in a matter of seconds Henry was spread out on the hood of the car, Samuel's automatic in his ear.

"Hey!" Henry yelled out. The paper bag was on the sidewalk, burst open and spreading out empty aluminum cans. Miller stood outside, touched at the sight of the cans rolling away, knowing the few cents Henry was going to get for turning them in. Miller was glad at the chance of being able to stand up and be outside, but he hated the look on the boy's face. Henry wet his lips and his hands were shaking and Jacob came over and patted him down.

Jacob stood back, his own pistol in his hand. "He's clean."

"Hey, come on, what's going on, what do you want?" he said, his voice trembling, the pitch much higher.

"Haven't you figured it?" Samuel asked, backing away and moving quickly again, and then Henry's arms were handcuffed behind him. "We want you, sunshine."

The scent of smoke was an acrid burning at the back of his throat. Miller coughed and in a few seconds, Samuel had dragged the teenager to the rear seat of the car. Miller clambered in the front seat and all the doors seemed to slam at once. Jacob threw the car into drive and sped out into the dirty street. Miller turned around. Henry Williams seemed to have shrunk within himself but his eyes were full of life and fear. Samuel had a wide grin on his sweaty face. His pistol was hidden away.

"Told you," Samuel said. "Piece of cake. Make that one hundred and one."

Jacob said, his voice quiet, "You shouldn't count that girl."

"Don't worry. At least I can count and read. Man, let's wrap this one up so we can eat. I'm starving."

Henry leaned forward and said, his voice desperate, "But I didn't do anything."

"Relax," Samuel said, pushing him gently back into the seat. "Everybody says that. Everybody."

Miller turned around again, his stomach queasy, the body armor making him feel like he weighed a thousand pounds. They sped by the two burning buildings and he caught a quick glance, of a circle of youths, dancing in a circle of flames, holding up their weapons in triumph. He wondered what their eyes looked like.

At the old precinct house they parked in a lower level garage and he said, "Room seven," and then took the stairs to his third-floor cube. The elevator was not to be trusted, and after tonight's pick-up, he didn't want to miss the interrogation because he was stuck between floors. That was a type of thing that would not look so hot on his six-month evaluation sheet and even through all his time with street work, he still cared about those evaluation reports.

On the west side of the third floor two large offices had been subdivided into cubicles. There were others working there but he ignored them as he went into his own work area. This was supposedly a temporary assignment. He wasn't one for making friendships that didn't last, that didn't count.

His cube was nine feet to a square, and contained filing cabinets, a battered desk, a swivel chair that squeaked no matter how many times it was lubricated, and a data processing terminal that crashed every time it rained outside. He stripped off the body armor, feeling light-headed at the sensation of the weights being removed and enjoying the scratching sound of the Velcro releases being pulled away. He threw the armor in the bottom drawer of one of the filing cabinets and sat down on his chair and looked out the grilled window. Not much of a view. Some other darkened buildings and a smidgen of the night sky. Still, it was a window view, and on the third floor, that meant something. He put his feet up on the windowsill and without looking behind him, reached over and picked up the framed photo.

He held the photograph in his lap and let himself smile a bit. The only piece of personal property he had allowed himself to bring to this office. It was a picture of Amy, wearing a small black bathing suit and sitting in the cockpit of a sailing boat, a tiller in her tanned hands. She wore sunglasses and was smiling, and her hair was pulled back in a ponytail. It had been taken last summer at a small port village in Maine. When this duty had come up she had frowned and said, of course she would wait, because this duty station was not one for many days off and she wasn't about to follow him here. There had been letters and some phone calls and some late nights, slightly drunk, when he forced himself to try to remember how it felt, spreading suntan oil on her back, laughing and feeling summer breezes over his skin.

That was then, when he made a home in a condo on the cool Atlantic, within easy driving distance to work and there was a silence at night that only echoed with the sounds of the ocean's waves. He now lived in a small apartment building that was guarded and contained only his co-workers, and on nights like these, Maine and Amy seemed thousands of miles away.

His phone rang. He sighed and dropped his feet and returned the photo to his desk. He picked up the phone and said, "Yes?"

"Henry Williams is waiting for you, Mr. Miller. Room seven."

"I'll be right down." After hanging up the phone he reached out and stroked the photo for a moment, and then left his cubicle.

The door to room seven clicked shut behind him and Miller went in a few steps, carrying Henry Williams' file in his hands. The youth sat at a long wooden table, his hands folded before him, and as Miller came in, Henry jerked his head away from where he had been looking, at the other end of the table. At that end of the table was a complex of computer equipment. The walls were painted a dull yellow and were blank, and the ceiling tiles were stained from cigarette smoke.

Miller nodded and sat down across from Henry. The boy's eyes were still alive, though angry and confused. The bright look in those eyes encouraged him for a moment.

"Man, I didn't do anything," he announced. "Why in hell did you guys roust me?"

"Because of some things you have done, Henry," Miller said.

"Hunh," he said, sitting back, his hands still folded together, and he snuck another glance at the computer equipment. "Like what? I'm clean."

"So you are." Miller opened up the file folder, started looking at the summary on the first page. "But you have been busy. You've got a near-perfect attendance record at your school. You're near the tops in your class. Your school had some fifteen-year-old computer equipment. Using some mail order supplies, you single-handedly upgraded the equipment, making it the best in the district. If you graduate in two years, you'll probably be your class valedictorian."

Henry snorted. "What do you mean, 'if.' Man, there's no

doubt about it. I am getting the hell and away from this place as soon as I can, with the best marks I can borrow or steal."

"And to what? Colleges? Things are tight everywhere, Henry. Grants and scholarship funds are being cut."

"I know. There's the service."

Miller shrugged. "Perhaps. But even the Defense Department has budget cutbacks, Henry. They've got enough problems keeping the soldiers they have in the service, without having to train new ones. Layoffs in the Army and Navy, if you can believe it. No, I was right before, Henry. If you graduate."

"And I was right, man," Henry said. "There's no 'if.' I am graduating."

"Like your friend last year, Tommy Sampson?"

Henry leaned forward. "What do you know about Tommy?"

"About him and what happened to him. What you are in computers, Tommy was in chemistry. A genius, right? And when he was seventeen, he went to a market for some groceries for his mother and got in the way of an armed robbery. A genius, Henry, a smart one like you, and instead of doing something with that he was cut down by a couple of thugs who couldn't even write their own names."

"Man," Henry whispered. "How come you cops know so much about me and Tommy?"

Miller raised an eyebrow. "Who ever said we were cops?"

After a few moments Miller folded his hands and said, "You're a prize, Henry. One of the bright ones that pop up every now and then. So you're going to understand me when I discuss a little history and current affairs."

"Hey, if you're not cops, then I want—"

He raised a hand. "Please. Give me a few minutes and

when we're done, you'll be free to go. We'll give you a car and a driver and he'll take you anywhere in the city. Just let me finish."

Miller took a deep breath, remembering the different classes he had taken and the drills he had gone through, all leading up to this moment, of trying to reach a very scared and very angry teenager. And trying to convince him or her of something.

"It's like this," he continued. "We're now fighting a world war, Henry, and we're losing. And we're losing to the two countries we beat back in 1945, and this time, we're losing not on the battlefield, but in the labs and boardrooms."

"Yeah?" he said, his voice sounding bored but his eyes betraying him. Henry was definitely interested.

"Yeah," Miller repeated. "We're getting beaten. Read the newspapers, watch the television. Japan and Germany are cooperating like never before, and they are taking great pleasure in humiliating us this time around. We're becoming second-class, maybe even third-class, and I've traveled abroad, Henry, and there's no fun in being a third-class country. Your life tends to be dirty, short, and miserable. There's a dozen, maybe even a hundred reasons why this happened, and one big one is what we're producing in our schools, Henry. Their high school seniors can work rings around our college graduate students, while the majority of our high school students can't tell you what century the Civil War was fought in."

"You're from the Department of Education, right? Feds."

Miller smiled. "Wrong. And I'll let you know in a moment who I do work for. But look at what I've just told you, and tell me, who would be the most concerned about what our schools were producing?"

"Parents, right?"

"Wrong again." Miller leaned forward again, looking intently into those bright eyes. "Businesses. Companies. Corporations. They all have one thing in common and that's in looking out for their best interests, the bottom line, the competition. And it's hard to do that, especially with overseas competition, when you can't fill jobs because your applicants can't complete an employment form. It's nothing new—companies for years have done what they can in helping high school graduates actually learn something after they get their diploma. Remedial classes. Workshops. Other programs, in anticipation someday that the courts, school boards and city governments would do something about the problem in the future. Well, they haven't, and each year, bigger and bigger chunks of the cities become free-fire zones. And each year, more and more of your classmates get killed, because they were in the wrong place."

"Thanks for the lecture," Henry said. "You're real bright, telling me something I don't know, that I live and go to school in a dump. So what are you, man? A social worker?"

Miller smiled. "I'm a thief. Like everyone else in this building."

"And what do you steal?"

"We steal the smart ones, Henry. I belong to a quiet little group formed by a number of corporations. We find out who's the very best, who's doing well in school, who has a future, and we go in and steal them. In some way it's a rescue mission, Henry. What use is it in trying to help someone after they graduate, when the best ones don't even make it to their graduation because they got caught in a drive-by shooting?"

"Some role model you are."

Miller said, "I'm not a role model, never pretended to be."

Henry glanced over at the computer equipment. "This

program must be some secret, I've never heard of it before. Even down here, mister, I read the newspapers."

"Then you're in the minority, Henry. Think it through. Of course it's a confidential program. It has to be. Think of the uproar in the media and the school boards, if they learned corporations were stealing the very best students and leaving everyone else behind."

Henry grunted. "Somebody in some boardroom must love secrets, come up with a program like that. Why don't you just donate money, get a school named after you?"

"Limited resources. And if you read the newspapers, you know where those donations end up, whose pockets they go to, and they don't end up helping students."

"You guys must have a big heart, to be interested in little ol' me."

Miller said, "Hearts have nothing to do with it, Henry. The bottom line does. Getting an edge on Japan and Germany, before they start electing our government."

Henry eased his head back, laughed. "Seems they could probably do a better job, the stuff I see down here every day."

Miller motioned to the computer equipment. "You see stuff like that down here?"

"It looks kinda familiar."

Miller said, "It's the latest Apple computer. The Cortland series. It's not even in the stores yet, won't be until this fall. But that's the type of equipment you'll be working with if you sign on with us." He motioned to the door. "There are other rooms on this floor. One has the latest video equipment. Another has a chem lab. And up on the roof, even some astronomy equipment, even though the light pollution is horrible. We show them to different students, depending on their interests. All examples of the very best, of what you'll be working with, if you sign on."

Henry touched his lips briefly with his tongue. "Tell me what sign on means."

He held out his hands. "There's a number of options. You drop out of your current school. Chances are, they won't miss you. Paperwork gets lost. You tell your family members anything that works, from moving to another city to transferring to another school. We'll help you with that. Then you get out of this city, to someplace safe, and you continue your education. Think of it as joining the service. We take care of all your education, and in return, we ask for a few years of your time. And throughout this all, Henry, you'll be working with the best."

"Just like that?"

"Just like that," Miller agreed.

"Man," Henry said. "Does it make you feel good, coming into the slums like this in your shiny car and new suit, and rescue some poor little boy from his fate? Show him all the fancy doodads and riches that's for him if he works for your corporations? That make you feel good? Does it?"

Miller felt like sighing. "No, it doesn't."

"Then why do you do it?"

"Because it's all I can do, that's why."

Henry looked miserable for a moment. "There are some good kids in my classes, you know. Kids who could use this help."

"We know. But we're losing. We only have time and resources to take out the very best."

Henry nodded. "And my uncle and aunt? They're the closest family I got."

"There's a stipend available . . . "

"Jeez, I don't know, I just don't know." Henry bit at his lip. "This is all happening so fast, you know? Suppose I say no? What then?"

Miller stood up and picked up the boy's file. "Then you can leave." He nodded to the computer equipment. "We'd prefer you don't tell anyone, but even if you do, well, who would believe you? You can even take the Cortland, if you'd like. Maybe you will make it on your own, Henry. But how good are the locks in your apartment? Word gets out that you have a system like that in your home . . . "

He didn't bother finishing the sentence. Henry was staring at the computer system, his eyes very bright indeed, and Miller nodded. Henry was his.

And as he left the room, he felt no triumph. Just a sickness.

They were back in the car again, Jacob and Samuel up front, and he in back, with another folder. This one said Tracy Cullen. The windows were down and the breeze with scent of smoke and trash was still there, as the car inched through the restaurant's parking lot. At the entrance to the lot there were two private security guards with shotguns who nodded at them as they drove in.

Samuel said, "It's amazing that his place stays open but boy, they have the best chicken sandwiches this side of the city. You hungry, Miller?"

He stared out the window. "Nope, I guess not. I'll have a Coke. That's all."

He shivered. He thought of what he saw and remembered where he had come from. Maine seemed like another universe, and his times there, a dream. This was reality. These loud streets and these kids. Warm summer days in Maine with Amy could not have existed, could not have happened.

Jacob stopped the car before a menu display and a young boy was there, holding a sheaf of papers. He handed one over to Jacob.

"Microphone for the drive-up's broke," the boy said. "Fill this out and I'll run it in."

Jacob took in the piece of paper and Samuel said, "Forget it, here, let me write it down."

"No," the boy said. "You gotta fill out the form."

Samuel scribbled something and said, "No, kid, here's our order. Now, run it in."

The boy frowned and ran away and Samuel said, "Three cheeseburgers for you, right, Jacob?"

Jacob nodded. "As always."

"And a Coke, Miller."

"That's right." He picked up the folder and brought it to his chest. The car inched forward and went to the drive-up window, and a man of about twenty leaned through the window. He had on a stained white uniform and had a knife scar on one cheek. He held out a blank sheet of paper.

"Sorry, man, you gotta fill out this menu sheet. It's the rules."

Jacob smiled at Samuel and Samuel snorted, reaching over and grabbing the sheet of paper, and then he grinned and held it up to Miller.

"See that? See what we're becoming?" On the sheet of paper were drawings of sandwiches and hamburgers, french fries and drinks. There were spaces underneath each drawing.

Samuel said, "No one can read in there. No one, man. You have to talk to them by using pictures, write little numbers under each menu item." He laughed and started writing on the sheet of paper. "Is this a great country or what?"

Miller looked into the restaurant and it seemed like all of the workers were looking at him for a moment, and their eyes were not like Henry Williams' at all. Their eyes were dead and they frightened him so, for there were so many of them, and he was all alone.

My favorite story, and one that has been the most widely anthologized and re-published. It was also my first sale to Playboy *magazine. It's a story of a man who's gone around the world, doing violent things for his country, and when it's time to retire and relax, he finds he's not welcome in his new home. For whatever reason, the oldtimers in his town don't accept him in their midst. The petty harassment starts and becomes more serious, and he's tempted to return to his violent ways to settle the situation. But being a smart fellow, he manages to get his revenge in a unique way.*

The Dark Snow

When I get to the steps of my lakeside home, the door is open. I slowly walk in, my hand reaching for the phantom weapon at my side, everything about me extending and tingling as I enter the strange place that used to be my home. I step through the small kitchen, my boots crunching the broken glassware and dishes on the tile floor. Inside the living room with its cathedral ceiling the furniture has been upended, as if an earthquake had struck.

I pause for a second, looking out the large windows and past the enclosed porch, down to the frozen waters of Lake Marie. Off in the distance are the snow-covered peaks of the White Mountains. I wait, trembling, my hand still curvng for that elusive weapon. They are gone, but their handiwork remains. The living room is a jumble of furniture, torn books and magazines, shattered pictures and frames. On one clear white plaster wall, right next to the fireplace, two words have been written in what looks to be ketchup: GO HOME.

This is my home. I turn over a chair and drag it to the windows. I sit and look out at the crisp winter landscape, legs stretched out, holding both hands quite still in my lap, which is quite a feat.

For my hands at that moment want to be wrapped around someone's throat.

After a long time wandering I came to Nansen, New Hampshire, in the late summer, and purchased a house right along the shoreline of Lake Marie. I didn't waste much time and I didn't bargain. I made an offer that was about a thousand dollars less than the asking price, and in less than a month it belonged to me.

At first I didn't know what to do with it. I had never had a residence that was actually mine. Everything else had been apartments, hotel rooms or temporary officer's quarters. The first few nights I couldn't sleep inside. I would go outside to the long dock that extends into the deep blue waters of the lake, bundle myself up in a sleeping bag and rested on a thin foam mattress, and lay back and stared up at the stars, and listened to the loons, getting ready for their long winter trip. The loons don't necessarily fly south; the ones here go out to the cold Atlantic and float with the waves and currents, not once touching land the entire winter.

As I snuggled in my bag I thought that was a good analogy for what I'd been doing. I had drifted for too long. It was time to come back to dry land.

After getting the power and other utilities up and running and moving in the few boxes of stuff that belonged to me, I checked the bulky envelope that accompanied my retirement and pulled out an envelope with a doctor's name. Inside the envelope were official papers that directed me to talk to him, and I shrugged and decided it was better than sitting here in an empty house, getting drunk. I phoned him and got an appointment for the next day.

His name is Ron Longley and he works in Manchester, the state's largest city and about an hour's drive south from Lake Marie. His office was in a refurbished brick building along the banks of the Merrimack River. I imagined I could still smell the sweat and toil of the French-Canadians who had worked here for so many years in the shoe, textile and leather mills, until their distant cousins in Georgia and Alabama took their jobs away.

I wasn't too sure what to make of Ron during our first session. He showed me some documents that made him a Department of Defense contractor and gave his current classification level, and then after signing the usual insurance nonsense, we got down to it. He was about ten years younger than me, with a mustache and not much hair on top. He wore jeans, a light blue shirt and a tie that looked like about six tubes of paint had been squirted onto it, and he said, "Well, here we are."

"That we are," I said. "And would you believe that I've already forgotten if you're a psychologist or a psychiatrist?"

That made for a good laugh. With a casual wave of his hand, he said, "Makes no difference. What would you like to talk about?"

"What should I talk about?"

A casual shrug, one of many I would eventually see. "Whatever's on your mind."

"Really?" I said, not bothering to hide the challenge in my voice. "Try this one on then, doc. I'm wondering what I'm doing here. And another thing I'm wondering is all that nice paperwork you have. Are you going to be making a report down south on how I do? You working under some deadline, some pressure?"

His hands were on his belly and he smiled. "Nope."

"Not at all?"

"Not at all," he said. "If you want to come in here and talk baseball for fifty minutes, then that's fine with me."

I looked at him and those eyes and maybe it's my change of view since retirement, but there was something trusting about him. I said, "You know what's really on my mind?"

"No, but I'd like to know."

"My new house," I said. "It's great. It's on a big lake and there aren't any close neighbors, and I can just sit on the dock at night and see stars I haven't seen in a long time. But I've been having problems sleeping."

"Why's that?" he asked, and I was glad he wasn't one of those stereotypical head docs, the ones who take a lot of notes.

"Weapons."

"Weapons?"

I nodded. "Yeah, I miss my weapons." A deep breath. "Look, you've seen my files, you know the places and the jobs that Uncle Sam has sent me to do. All those years, I had pistols or rifles or heavy weapons, always at my side, under my bed or in a closet. They helped me sleep. But when I moved in and started living in that house, well, I don't have them any more."

"How does that make you feel?" and even though the question was friendly, I knew it was a real doc question, and not a from-the-next-end-of-the-barstool type question.

I rubbed my hands. "I really feel like I'm changing my ways. But damn it . . . "

"Yes?"

I smiled. "I sure could use a good night's sleep."

As I drove back home, I thought, *Hell, it's only a little white lie.*

103

The fact is, I do have my weapons.

They were locked up in the basement, in strongboxes with heavy combination locks. I couldn't get to them quickly, but I certainly haven't tossed them away.

I hadn't been lying when I told Ron that I couldn't sleep. That part was entirely true.

I thought, as I drove up the dirt road to my house and scared a possum, scuttling along the side of the dirt and gravel, that the real problem was so slight that I was embarrassed to bring it up to Ron.

It was the noise.

I was living in a rural paradise, with clean air, clean water, and views of the woods and the lake and mountains that almost break my heart each time I climb out of bed, stiff with old dreams and old scars. The long days were filled with work and activities that I'd never had the time for. Cutting old brush and trimming dead branches. Planting annual bulbs for the next spring. Clearing my tiny beach of dead leaves and other debris. Filling bird feeders. And during the long evenings on the front porch or on the dock, I tackled thick history books.

But one night after dinner—and I'm surprising myself at finding that I'm beginning to enjoy cooking—I was out on the dock, sitting in one of those 1950's-era web lawnchairs, a glass of red wine in my hand and a history of the Apollo space program in my lap. Along the shoreline of Lake Marie, I could see lights of the cottages and other homes. Every night there were fewer and fewer lights, as more of the summer people boarded up their places and headed back to suburbia.

I was enjoying my wine and the book and the slight breeze, but there was also a distraction: three high-powered speedboats, racing around on the lake and tossing up great spumes of spray and noise. They were dragging people along the rear in inner-tubes and it was hard to concentrate on my book. After a while the engines slowed down and I was hoping that they were heading back to their docks, but the boats drifted together and ropes were exchanged, and soon, they became a large raft. A couple of grills were set up, and there were more hoots and yells, and then a sound system kicked in, with rock music and a heavy bass that echoed among the hills.

It was then too dark to read and I'd lost interest in the wine and I was sitting there, arms folded tight against my chest, trying hard to breathe. The noise got louder and I gave up and retreated into the house, where the heavy *thump-thump* of the bass followed me in. If I had a boat I could have gone out and asked them politely to turn it down, but that would have meant talking to many people and putting myself in the way, and I didn't want to do that.

Instead, I retreated upstairs to my bedroom and shut the door and windows, and still, that *thump-thump* shook through the very wood and beams of the house. I lay down, staring up, pillow about my head, and tried not to think of what's in the basement.

Later that night I got up for a drink of water, and there was still noise and music. I walked out to the porch and could see movement out on the lake, and hear laughter. On a tree near the dock is a spotlight that the previous owners had installed, and which I had rarely used, but at this hour in the morning, I flipped on the switch. Some shouts and a shriek. Two power boats, tied together, had drifted close to my shore. The light caught a young muscular man, with a fierce black moustache, standing on the stern of his powerboat and urinating into the lake. His half dozen companions, male and female, yelled and cursed in my direction. The boats started up and two men and a young woman stumbled to one side of a boat and dropped their bathing suits, exposing their buttocks. A couple of others gave me a one-fingered salute, and there was a shower of beer bottles and cans tossed over the side as they sped away.

I spent the next hour on the porch, staring into the darkness.

The next day, I made two phone calls, to the town hall and the police department of Nansen. I made gentle and polite inquiries, and got the same answers from each office. There's no local or state law about boats coming to within a certain distance of shore. There's also no law about mooring together. Nansen being such a small town, there was also no noise ordinance.

Home sweet home.

On my next visit Ron was wearing a bowtie. He said, "Still having sleeping problems?"

I was proud to be smiling. "No, not at all."

"Really?"

"It's fall," I said. "The tourists have gone home, most of the cottages along the lake have been boarded up, and nobody takes out boats anymore. It's so quiet at night I can hear the house creak and settle."

"That's good, that's really good," Ron said, and I changed the subject. A half-hour later, I was heading back to my new home in Nansen, thinking about another white lie I had just performed. Well, it wasn't really a lie. More of an oversight.

I hadn't told Ron about the hang-up phone calls. Or how trash had twice been dumped in my driveway. Or a week ago, when I was shopping, someone had drilled a bullet hole through one of the side windows. Maybe a hunting accident.

Even though hunting season wasn't yet open, I knew that for some of the working men in this town, it didn't matter when the state allows them to do their shooting.

I had cleaned up the driveway, shrugged off the phone calls, and cut away brush and saplings around the house, to eliminate any potential hiding spots for . . . hunters.

Still, I could sit out on the dock, a blanket around my legs and lap and a mug of tea in my hand, watching the sun set in the distance, the reddish pink highlighting the strong yellows, oranges and reds of the foliage. The water was a slate gray and though I missed the loons, the smell of the leaves and the tang of wood smoke from my chimney seemed to settle in just fine.

As it grew colder, I began going to downtown Nansen for breakfast every few days. The center of Nansen could be featured in a documentary on New Hampshire small towns. Around the small green common with its Civil War statue in the center are a bank, real estate office, hardware store, two service stations, a general store, a small strip of stores that has everything from a plumber to a video rental place, and Gretchen's Kitchen. At Gretchen's I read the papers while letting the morning drift by. I listened to the old timers sit at the counter and pontificate on the ills of the state, nation, and world, and watched harried workers fly in to grab a quick meal. Eventually a waitress named Sandy took some interest in me.

She was about twenty years younger than I, with raven hair, a wide smile, and a pleasing body that filled out her regulation pink uniform. After a couple of weeks of serious flirting and generous tips on my part, I actually asked her out, and when she said yes, I went out to my pickup truck and burst out laughing. A real date. I couldn't remember the last time I had actually had a real date.

The first date was dinner a couple of towns over in Montcalm, the second was dinner and a movie outside of Manchester, and the third was a homemade dinner at my house that was supposed to end with a rented movie in the living room, but instead ended up in the bedroom. Along the way I learned that Sandy had always lived in Nansen, was divorced with two young boys, and was saving up her money so she could go back to school and become a legal aide. "If you think I'm going to keep on slinging hash and waiting for Billy to remember to send his support check, then you're a damn fool," she said on our first date.

After a bedroom interlude that surprised me with its intensity, we sat on the enclosed porch. I opened a window for Sandy since she needed a smoke. The house was warm and I had on a pair of shorts; she had wrapped a towel around her torso. I sprawled out in an easy chair while she sat on the couch, feet in my lap. Both of us had glasses of wine and I felt comfortable and tingling. Sandy glanced at me as she worked on her cigarette. I'd left the lights off and lit up a couple of candles, and in the hazy yellow light, I made out a small tattoo of a unicorn on her right shoulder.

Sandy looked at me and asked, "What were you doing when you was in the government?"

"Traveled a lot and ate bad food."

"No, really," she said. "I want a straight answer."

Well, I thought, as straight as I can be without violating certain agreements, and I said, "I was a consultant, to foreign armies. Sometimes they needed help in using certain weapons or training techniques. That was my job."

"Were you good?"

Too good, I thought. "I did all right."

"You've got a few scars there."

"That I do."

She shrugged, took a lazy puff off her cigarette. "I've seen worse."

I wasn't sure where this was headed. Then she said, "When are you going to be leaving?"

Confused, I said, "You mean, tonight?"

"No," she said. "I mean, when are you leaving Nansen, and going back home." I looked around the porch and I said, "This is my home."

She gave me a slight smile, like a teacher correcting a fumbling but eager student. "No, it's not. This place was built by the Gerrish family. It's the Gerrish place. You're from away, and this ain't your home."

I tried to smile, though my mood was slipping. "Well, I beg to disagree."

She said nothing for a moment, just studying the trail of smoke from her cigarette. Then she said, "Some people in town don't like you. They think you're uppity, a guy that don't belong here."

I began to find it quite cool on the porch. "What kind of people?"

"The Garr brothers. Jerry Tompkins. Kit Broderick. A few others. Guys in town. They don't particularly like you."

"I don't particularly care," I shot back.

A small shrug, as she stubbed out her cigarette. "You will."

The night crumbled some more after that, and the next morning, while sitting in the corner at Gretchen's, I was ignored by Sandy. One of the older waitresses served me, and my coffee arrived in a cup stained with lipstick, the bacon was charred black and the eggs were cold. I got the message and started making my own breakfast at home, sitting alone on the porch, watching the leaves fall and days grow shorter.

I wondered if Sandy was on her own or if she had been

scouting out enemy territory on someone's behalf.

At my December visit, I surprised myself by telling Ron of something that had been bothering me.

"It's the snow," I said, leaning forward, hands clasped between my legs. "I know that it's going to start snowing soon. And I've always hated the snow, especially since . . . "

"Since when?"

"Since something I did once," I said. "In Serbia."

"Go on," he said, fingers making a tent in front of his face.

"I'm not sure if I can."

Ron tilted his head quizzically. "You know I have the clearances."

I cleared my throat, my eyes burning a bit. "I know. It's just that it's. . . . Ever see blood on snow, at night?"

I had his attention. "No," he said, "no, I haven't."

"It steams at first, since it's so warm," I said. "And then it gets real dark, almost black. Dark snow, if you can believe it. It's something that stays with you, always."

He looked steadily at me for a moment, then said, "Do you want to talk about it some more?"

"No."

I spent all of one gray afternoon in my office cubby-hole, trying to get a new computer up and running. When at last I went downstairs for a quick drink, I looked outside and there they were, big snowflakes, la-zily drifting to the ground. Forgetting about the drink, I went out to the porch and looked at the pure whiteness of everything, of the snow covering the bare limbs, the shrubbery, and the frozen lake. I stood there and hugged myself and saw the softly accumulating blanket of white, and feeling lucky.

★ ★ ★ ★ ★

Two days after the snowstorm I was out on the frozen waters of Lake Marie, breathing hard and sweating and enjoying every second of it. The day before I had driven into Manchester and had gone to a sporting goods store, and had come out with a pair of cross-country skis. The air was crisp and still, and the sky was a blue so deep I half-expected to see brushstrokes. From the lake I looked back and saw my home and I liked what I saw. The white paint and plain construction made me smile for no particular reason.

I heard not a single sound, except for the faint drone of a distant airplane. Before me someone had placed signs in the snow and orange colored ropes, covering an oval area in about the center of the lake. Each sign said the same thing: DANGER! THIN ICE! I remembered hearing the old timers at Gretchen's Kitchen telling a story about a hidden spring coming up through the lake bottom, or some damn thing, that always made the center of the lake thin with ice, even in the coldest weather. I got cold and it was time to go home.

About halfway back to the house is when it happened.

At first it was a quiet sound, and I thought that it was another airplane. Then the noise got louder and louder, and separated, becoming distinct. Engines, several of them. I turned and they came out of the woods, speeding out into the snow, tossing up great rooster tails of snow and ice. Snowmobiles, an even half dozen, and they were heading straight for me. I turned away and kept on my steady pace, trying to shut out the growing loudness of the approaching engines. There was an itchy feeling crawling up my spine to the base of my head, and the loud noise exploded in pitch as they raced by me.

Even with the loudness of the engines I could make out

the yells as the snowmobiles roared by, tossing snow in my direction. There were two people to each machine and they didn't look human. Each one was dressed in a bulky, zippered jumpsuit, heavy boots and padded motorcycle crash helmets. They raced by and sure enough, they circled around and came back at me. This time I flinched. This time, too, a couple of empty beer cans were thrown my way.

By the third pass I was getting closer to my house. I thought it was almost over when one of the snowmobiles broke free from the pack and raced across about fifty feet in front of me. The driver turned so that the machine was blocking me, and he sat there, racing the throttle. Then he pulled off his helmet, showing an angry face and thick mustache, and I recognized the man from a few months ago, the one with the powerboat. He handed his helmet to his passenger, stepped off the snowmobile, and unzipped his jumpsuit. It only took a moment, as he marked the snow in a long, steaming stream, and then there was laughter from the others as he got back on the machine, and sped away. I skied over the soiled snow, and forced myself to take my time climbing up the snow-covered lakeshore and entered my home, carrying my skis and poles like weapons over my shoulders.

That night, and every night afterward, they came back, breaking the winter stillness with the throbbing sounds of engines, laughter, drunken shouts, and music from portable stereos. Each morning I got up and cleaned out their debris and scuffed fresh snow over the stains, and in the quiet of my house, I found myself constantly on edge, always listening, always waiting for the noises of the engines to suddenly return and break up the day. A couple of more phone calls to the police department and the town hall reconfirmed what I already knew: except for maybe littering, no ordinances or laws were being broken.

On one particularly loud night I broke a promise to myself and went to the tiny and damp cellar, to undo a combination lock to a green metal case and take out a pistol-shaped device. I went back upstairs to the enclosed porch and with all of the lights off, I switched on the night vision scope and looked at the scene below me. Six snowmobiles were parked in a circle on the snow-covered ice and in the center, a fire had been set. Figures stumbled around in the snow, talking and laughing, and throwing beer cans in all directions. Portable stereos had been set up on the seats of two of the snowmobiles and the loud music with its bass *thump-thump-thump* echoed and re-echoed across the flat ice. Lake Marie is one of the largest bodies of water in this part of the county, but they always set up camp right below my windows.

I watched for a while as they partied. Two of the black-suited figures started wrestling in the snow. More shouts and laughter, and then the fight broke up and someone turned the stereos up even louder. *Thump-thump-thump.*

I switched off the night vision scope and returned it to its case in the cellar, and then went to bed. Even with foam rubber earplugs in my ears, the bass noise reverberated inside my skull. I put the pillow across my face and tried to ignore the whispers inside of me, the ones that tell me to get used to it, that this will continue all winter, the noise and the littering and the aggravation, and when spring comes, they'll just turn in their snowmobiles for boats, and they'll be back out here, all summer long.

Thump-thump-thump.

At the next session with Ron we talked about the weather

until he pierced me with his gaze and said, "Tell me what's wrong."

I went through a half-dozen rehearsals of what to tell him, and then I skated to the edge of the truth and said, "I'm having a hard time adjusting, that's all."

"Adjusting to what?"

"To my home," I said, my hands clasped before me. "I never thought I would say this, but I'm really beginning to get settled, for the first time in my life. You ever been in the military, Ron?"

"No, but I know—"

I held up my hand. "Yes, I know what you're going to say. You've worked as a consultant but you've never been one of us, Ron. Never. You never know what it's like, being ordered about, being told to go here and live in a place for a year, and then uproot yourself and go halfway across the world to a place with different language, customs, and weather, all within a week. You never really settle in, never really get into a place you call home."

He swiveled a bit in his black leather chair. "But that's different now."

"It sure is," I said.

There was a pause, as we looked at each other, and Ron said, "But something is going on."

"Something certainly is."

"Tell me."

And then I knew I wouldn't. A fire wall had been set up between my sessions with Ron and the details of what was going on back at my home. If I let him know what's really happening, I knew that he would make a report, and within the week, I'd be ordered to go somewhere else. If I was younger and not so dependent on a monthly check, I would put up a fight.

But now, no more fighting. I looked past Ron and said, "An adjustment problem, I guess."

"Adjusting to civilian life?"

"More than that," I said. "Adjusting to living in Nansen. It's a great little town, but . . . I still feel like an outsider."

"That's to be expected."

"Sure, but I still don't like it. I know it will take some time, but . . . well, I get the odd looks, the quiet little comments, the cold shoulders."

Ron seemed to choose his words carefully. "Is that proving to be a serious problem?"

Not even a moment of hesitation, as I lied: "No, not at all."

"And what do you plan on doing?"

An innocent shrug. "Not much. Just try to fit in, try to be a good neighbor."

"That's all?"

I nodded firmly. "That's all."

It took a bit of research but eventually I managed to get a name to the face of the mustached man who had pissed on my territory. Jerry Tompkins. A floor supervisor for a computer firm outside of Manchester, married with three kids, and an avid boater, snowmobiler, hunter, and all-around guy. His family has been in Nansen for generations and his dad is one of the three selectmen who run the town. Using a couple of old skills I tracked him down, and pulled my truck next to his in the snowy parking lot of a tavern on the outskirts of Nansen on a dark afternoon. The tavern was called Peter's Pub and the windows were barred and blacked out.

I stepped out of my truck and called out to him, as he walked to the entrance of the pub. He turned and glared at me. "What?"

"You're Jerry Tompkins, aren't you."

"Sure am," he said, hands in the pocket of his dark green parka. "And you're the fella that's living up in the old Gerrish place."

"Yes, and I'd like to talk to you for a second."

His face was a bit rough, like he had spent a lot of times outdoors, in the wind and rain, and an equal amount indoors, with cigarette smoke and loud country music. He rocked back on his heels with a little smile and said, "Go ahead. You got your second."

"Thanks," I said. "Tell you what, Jerry, I'm looking for something."

"And what's that?"

"I'm looking for a treaty."

He nodded, squinted his eyes. "What kind of treaty?"

"A peace treaty. Let's cut out the snowmobile parties on the lake by my place and the trash dumped in the driveway and the hang-up phone calls. Let's start fresh and just stay out of each other's way. What do you say? Then, this summer, you can all come over to my place for a cookout. I'll even supply the beer."

He rubbed at the bristles along his chin. "Seems like a one-sided deal. Not too sure what I get out of it."

"What's the point in what you're doing now?"

A furtive smile. "It suits me, that's why."

I felt like I'm beginning to lose it. "You agree with the peace treaty, we all win."

"Still don't see what I get out of it," he said.

"That's the purpose of a peace treaty," I said. "You get peace."

"Feel pretty peaceful right now."

"That might change," I said, instantly regretting the words.

His eyes darkened. "You threatening me?"

A retreat, recalling my promise to myself when I came here. "No, not a threat, Jerry. What do you say?"

He turned and walked away, moving his head to keep in view. "Your second got used up a long time ago, pal. And you better be out of this lot in another minute, or I'm going inside and coming out with a bunch of my friends. You won't like that."

No, I wouldn't, and it wouldn't be for the reason Jerry believed. If they did come out I'd be forced into old habits and old actions, and I'd promised myself I wouldn't do that. I couldn't.

"You got it," I said, backing away. "But remember this, Jerry. Always."

"What's that?"

"The peace treaty," I said, going to the door of my pickup truck. "I offered."

Another visit to Ron's, on a snowy day. The conversation sort of meandered along and I didn't know what got into me, for I turned to the old mill windows and looked outside and said, "What do people expect, anyway?"

"What do you mean?" he asked.

"You take a tough teenager from a small Ohio town, and you train him and train him and train him. You turn him into a very efficient hunter, a very efficient meat eater. Then, after twenty or thirty years, you say thank you very much and send him back to the world of quiet vegetarians, and you expect him to start eating cabbages and carrots with no fuss nor muss. A hell of a thing, thinking you can send a hunter home without any problems, expect him to put away his tools and skills."

"Maybe that's why we're here," he suggested.

117

"Oh, please," I said. "Do you think this makes a difference?"

"Does it make a difference to you?"

I kept on looking outside the window. "Too soon to tell, I'd say. Truth is, I wonder if this is meant to work, or is meant to make some people less guilty. The people who did the hiring, training and discharging."

"What do you think?"

I turned to him. "I think for the amount of money you charge Uncle Sam, you ask too many damn questions."

Another night at two a.m. I'm back outside of the porch, again with the night vision scope in my hands. They were back, and if anything, the music and the engines blared even louder. A fire burned merrily among the snowmobiles, and as they pranced and hollered, I wondered if some base part of their brains were remembering thousand-year-old rituals. As I looked at their dancing and drinking figures, I kept thinking of the long case at the other end of the cellar. Nice heavy-duty assault rifle with the same night vision scope, except this one has crosshairs. Scan and track. Put a crosshair across each one of their chests. Feel the weight of a fully-loaded magazine in your hands. Know that with a silencer on the end of the rifle, you could take out that crew in a fistful of seconds. Get your mind back into the realms of possibilities, of cartridges and windage and grains and velocities. Figure out what it would take. How long could it take, between the time you said go and the time you could say mission accomplished? Not long at all.

"No," I whispered back, switching off the scope. "Can't do it. Can't go back."

I stayed in the porch for another hour, and as my eyes adjusted, I saw more movements. I picked up the scope. A couple of snowmachines moved in, each with shapes on the seats, behind the driver. They pulled up to the snowy bank and the people moved quickly, intent on their work. Trash bags were tossed up on my land, about eight or nine, and to add a bit more fun, each bag was slit several times with a knife beforehand, so it could burst open and spew its contents when it hits the my land. A few more hoots and hollers and the snowmobiles growled away, leaving trash and the still flickering fire behind. I watched the lights as the snowmobiles roared across the lake, and finally disappeared, though their sound did not.

The night vision scope went back into my lap. The whisper returned: You could have stopped it right there, with a couple of rounds through the engines. Highly illegal but it would get their attention, right?

Right.

In my next session with Ron, I got to the point. "What kind of reports are you sending south?"

I think I might have surprised him. "Reports?"

"Sure. Stories about my progress, how I'm adjusting, that sort of thing."

He paused for a moment, and I knew there must be a lot of figuring going on behind those smiling eyes. "Just the usual things, that's all. That you're doing fine."

"Am I?"

"Seems so to me."

"Good." I waited for a moment, letting the words twist about on my tongue for a moment. "Then you can send them this message. I haven't been a hundred percent with you during these sessions, Ron, not by a long shot. Guess it's not in my nature to be so open. But you can count on this. I won't lose it. I won't go into a gun shop and come out and take down a bunch of civilians. I'm not going to start hanging around 1600 Pennsylvania Avenue. I'm going to be all right."

He smiled. "I've never had any doubt."

"Sure you've had doubts," I said, smiling back. "But that's awfully polite of you to say, anyway."

On a bright Saturday, I tracked down the police chief of Nansen at one of the two service stations in town, Glen's Gas & Repair. His cruiser, ordinarily a dark blue, was parked near the pumps and was now a ghostly shade of white from the road salt that's used to keep the roads clear. I parked at the side of the garage and in walking by the service bays, I could sense that I was being watched. I looked in to see some work going on around three cars with their hoods up, and I also saw a familiar uniform: black snowmobile jumpsuits.

The chief was overweight and wearing a heavy blue uniform jacket with a black Navy watchcap, but his face was open and friendly, and he nodded in all the right places as I told him my story.

"Not much I can do, I'm afraid," he said, leaning against the door of his cruiser, one of two in the entire town. "I'd have to catch 'em in the act of trashing your place, and that means a surveillance, and that means overtime hours, which I don't have."

"Let's be straight, chief. Any surveillance would be a waste of time. These guys, they aren't thugs, right? For lack of a better phrase, they're good ol' boys, and they know everything that's going on in Nansen, and they'd know if you were setting up a surveillance. And then they wouldn't show."

"You might think you're insulting me, but you're not," he said, gently. "That's just the way things are done here. It's a good town and most of us get along, and I'm not kept that busy, not at all."

"I appreciate that, but you should also appreciate my problem," I said. "I live here and I pay property taxes, and a group of men are harassing me. I'm looking for some assistance, that's all, and a suggestion of what I can do."

"You could move," the chief said, raising his coffee cup up.

"Hell of a suggestion."

"Best one I could come up with. Look, friend, you're new here, you've got no family, no ties. You're asking me to take on some prominent families here just because you and they don't get along. So why don't you move on? Find someplace even smaller, hell, even find someplace bigger, where you don't stand out that much. But face it. You don't belong in Nansen, and it's not going to be any easier."

"Real nice folks, then," I said, letting an edge of bitterness into my voice.

That didn't seem to bother the chief. "That they are. They work hard and play hard and pay taxes, and they look out for each other. I know those snowmobilers look like hellraisers to you, but they're more than that. They're part of the community. Why, just next week, a bunch of them are going on a midnight snow run across the lake and into the mountains, raising money for the children's camp up at Lake Montcalm. People who don't care about each other wouldn't do that."

"I just wish they didn't care so much about me."

He shrugged and said, "Look, I'll see what I can do . . . " but the tone of his voice made it clear he wasn't going to do a damn thing.

The chief clambered into his cruiser and drove off, and I walked past the open bays of the service station. I heard snickers. I went around to my pickup truck and saw the source of the merriment.

My truck, resting heavily on four flat tires.

At night I woke up from cold and bloody dreams and lay there, letting my thoughts drift into fantasies. By now I knew who all of them are, where all of them lived. I could go to their houses and take them out, every single one of them, and bring them back and bind them in the basement of my home. I could tell them who I was and what I've done and what I can do, and I would ask them to leave me alone. That's it. Just give me peace and solitude and everything would be all right.

A wonderful fantasy, that they would hear me out and nod and do what I say, but I knew that I would have to do more to convince them. So I would go to Jerry Tompkins, the moustached one who enjoys marking his territory, and to make my point, break a couple of his fingers, the popping noise echoing in the dark confines of the tiny basement.

Nice fantasies.

I asked Ron, "What's the point?"

He was comfortable in his chair, hands clasped over a little potbelly. "I'm sorry?"

"The point of our little sessions."

His eyes were unflinching. "To help you adjust."

"Adjust to what?"

"To civilian life."

I shifted some on the couch. "Let me get this. I work my entire life for this country, doing service for its civilians. I expose myself to death and injury every week, making about a third of what I could be doing in the private sector. All of this, and when I'm through, I'm told that I have to adjust, that I have to make allowances for civilians. But civilians, they don't have to do a damn thing. Is that right?"

"I'm afraid so."

"Hell of a deal."

He continued the steady gaze. "Only one you've got."

So here I am, in the smelly rubble that used to be my home. I make a few half-hearted attempts to turn the furniture back over and do some clean up work, but I'm not in the mood. Old feelings and emotions are coursing through me, are taking control. I take a few deep breaths and then I'm in the cellar, switching on the single light bulb, hanging down from the rafters by a frayed black cord. As I work among the packing cases and undo the combination locks, my shoulders strike the light bulb, causing it to swing back and forth, casting crazy shadows on the stone walls.

The night air is cool and crisp, and I shuffle through the snow around the house as I go out to the pickup truck, making three trips in all. I drive under the speed limit and halt completely at all stop signs as I go through the center of town, and as I drive around, wasting minutes and hours, listening to the radio. This late at night and being so far north, a lot of the stations I pick up are from Quebec, and there's a joyous nature to the French-Canadian music and words that make something inside of me ache with longing.

When it's almost a new day, I drive down a street called Mast Road. Most towns around here all have a Mast Road, where colonial surveyors would mark tall pines that would eventually become masts for the Royal Navy. Tonight there are no surveyors, just the night air and darkness and a skinny rabbit, racing across the cracked asphalt. When I'm near the target, I switch off the lights and engine and let the truck glide the last few hundred feet or so. I pull up across from a darkened house. A pickup truck and Subaru station wagon are in the driveway. Gray smoke is wafting up from the chimney.

I roll down the window, the cold air washing over me, almost like a wave of water. I pause, remembering what has gone on these past weeks, and then I get to work.

The night vision scope comes up and clicks into action, and the name on the mailbox is clear enough in the sharp green light. TOMPKINS, in silver and black stick-on letters picked up at the local hardware store. I scan the two-story Cape Cod, checking out the surroundings. There's an attached garage to the right, and a sunroom off to the left. There is a main door in front and two other doors in a breezeway that runs from the garage to the house. There are no rear doors.

I let the night scope rest in my lap and reach my hand over to the side, to my weapons. The first is a grenade launcher, with a handful of white phosphorus rounds clustered next to it on the seat, like a gathering of metal eggs. Next to the grenade launcher is a 9mm Uzi, with extended wooded stock for easier use. Another night vision scope with crosshairs is attached to the Uzi.

Another series of deep breaths. Easy enough plan. Pop a white phosphorus round into the breezeway and another into the sunroom. In a minute or two both ends of the house are on fire. Our snowmobiler friend and his family wake up, and groggy from sleep and the fire and the terror of the noise, they stumble out of the front door onto the snow-covered lawn.

And the Uzi is in my hand, and the crosshairs are on a certain face, a face with a moustache, and then I take care of business and drive on to the next house.

Sure.

I pick up the grenade launcher and rest the barrel on the open window. It's cold. I rub my legs together and look outside, up at the stars. The wind comes up and some snow blows across the road. I hear the low hoo-hoo-hoo of an owl.

I bring the grenade launcher up, resting the stock against my cheek. I aim. I wait.

It's very cold.

The weapon begins trembling in my hands, and then I let it drop to the front seat. "Fool," I whisper to myself. "Damn rookie."

I sit on my hands, trying to warm them up, and the breeze continues to blow. Idiot. Do this and how long before we're in jail, and how long after that are we on trial, before a jury full of friends or relatives of those fine citizens you gun down tonight?

I start up the truck and let the heater sigh itself on, and then I roll up the window and slowly drive away, lights still off.

Days later, there's a fresh smell to the air, for I've done a lot of cleaning and painting, trying not only to bring every-thing back to where it was, but also to spruce up the place. The only real problem was in the main room, where the words GO HOME were done in bright red ketchup on the white plaster wall. It's taken me three coats of paint to cover that up, and of course, I ended up doing the entire room.

The house is dark and it's late and I'm waiting, a glass of wine in my hand, standing on the porch, looking out to the frozen waters of Lake Marie, watching the light snow fall. Every light in the house is off and the only illumination comes from the fireplace, which is slowly dying and which needs some more wood.

But I'm content to dawdle. I'm finally at peace after these difficult weeks in Nansen. Finally, I'm beginning to re-member who I really am.

I sip my wine, waiting, and then comes the sound of the snowmobiles. I see their wavering dots of light, racing across the lake, doing their bit for charity. How wonderful. I raise my glass in salute, the noise of the snowmobiles getting a bit louder as they head across the lake in a straight line.

I then put the wineglass down and then walk into the living room, and toss the last few pieces of wood onto the fire, the sudden heat warming my face in a pleasant glow. The wood I toss in isn't firewood, though. It's been shaped and painted by man, and as the flames leap up and devour the lumber, I see the letters begin to fade: DANGER! THIN ICE!

I stroll back to the porch, pick up the wineglass, and wait.

Below me, on the peaceful and quiet shores of Lake Marie, my new home for my new life, the lights go by.

And then, one by one, they blink out, and the silence is wonderful.

The very first story I wrote for Martin Greenberg and his merry gang of anthologists. The collection this appeared in—"Once Upon a Crime"—is a collection of mystery stories that are based, one way or another, on fairy tales. At first I balked at the request—fairy tales?— but once I started thinking about it, I came up with a fun story that fit the bill.

Rapunzel's Revenge

Beside her Clem Tyson said in a low voice, "Well, it doesn't look like a castle."

Marie Celluci tried not to sigh in frustration. She stood with Clem in Quebec City on a wide and long boardwalk called Terrasse Dufferin and before them was an enormous building made of red brick, with dull copper green roofs and turrets and skylights and ramparts. It dominated this point of land that overlooked the St. Lawrence River and at this moment, one room in that building to her was the most important room in the world. Unlike many of the people on the boardwalk this early summer evening, they stood still. Around them, tourists moved about them, laughing and smiling and holding hands and taking photographs and watching the street performers juggle and perform tricks. She ignored them all. She looked at the quiet windows. Hundreds of windows, it seemed. *Just one,* she thought. Just one.

She said, "It's called a chateau. In French, chateau means castle. Believe me, Clem, it's a castle."

He shrugged. He was a few years younger than she and a bit shorter, and he favored tight, short-sleeve shirts that highlighted his hours in the gym. His thick hair was combed back with some sort of petroleum-based product, and he had a tiny mustache that he preened whenever he thought she wasn't looking.

Clem said, "Hell, I've seen the movies and television shows, you know? Castles got drawbridges. This one ain't got a drawbridge. So how come they call it a castle?"

Around her the tourists flowed and ebbed, like a slow-moving river of people. Everyone looked happy. She could not remember the last time she could have said that word about herself. Many of the visitors stopped to look at the street-performers, mimes and clowns and tricksters that performed feats of magic for the applauding crowds. *Tricksters,* she thought, looking over at Clem. *I need a trickster and this is what I get.*

And what do you expect, on a cop's salary?

"They call it a castle because they want to," she said gently. "If they wanted to call it a Superdome, I really wouldn't care. All I know is that Greg is in one of those rooms and we've got to get him out, and I want to know what ideas you have."

He smiled, showing teeth that hadn't been to a dentist lately. "Hon, I've got some ideas, don't you worry." He laughed. "Some of them even involve springing your husband. So don't fret yourself, we'll get him out."

A joke, she thought. *He thinks this whole mess is a joke, or an adventure, or, God help us, a quest. That's right. A quest, to rescue the one I love from a castle guarded by the forces of evil.* Despite all of it, she laughed, and Clem looked at her, smiling himself though a bit puzzled, she could see, at what possibly was so funny.

"Let's go eat," she said. "And then you'll tell me what you've got planned."

"For the rescue or for later?" he said, leering.

"Rescue first," she said, resisting an urge to use one of the three take-down holds she knew to toss him to the ground and knee him in the groin. "We get Greg out and everything else is negotiable."

What struck Greg Celluci so much—despite the moments of sheer terror every now and then—was how blessedly polite the three men could be whenever they wanted. Eventually he learned their names—Tony was the skinny one, Carlos was the pudgy one who could move so fast when he wanted to, and Paulie was the older one, and the leader. Tony and Carlos would lounge around in polo shirts and designer jeans, but Paulie would wear a suit and tie. Paulie also reported directly every day to Mr. Carmichael, and while in the past couple of weeks, both Tony and Carlos had caused him pain—his left forefinger and knee throbbed in memory of those dreadful few seconds—Paulie was the one that scared him the most. It was the eyes. Looking into those eyes was like looking into the rooms of an empty house.

He was in a luxurious room on the third floor of the Chateau Frontenac, and his room had a window overlooking a park—Governor's Park, it was called—and beside his bed there was a makeshift work area, with computers, terminals, keyboards, cables, modems, and phone lines. He was never left alone, except for sleeping at night. Right now, Tony was stretched out on the bed, working a crossword puzzle from a crossword puzzle digest. Greg could nap, watch television—and see *Baywatch* dubbed in French, which despite his circumstances was kind of amusing—and order every type of meal from room service. In some way, for a confirmed gear head like himself, it was bliss. All the computer time, long distance time and free room service food he could want. It was heaven. Save for two things, of course. One was Marie.

The other was the ability to walk out the door.

He had pled and had argued and had even threatened a strike, all for just the privilege of getting outside for a walk around the city and some fresh air, and Paulie had sat him down in another one of the suite's rooms and had gently explained the facts of life for him. He, Greg, was to stay in this room until his task for Mr. Carmichael was complete, and then, and only then would the situation change. And, to ensure that Greg never forgot this, Paulie had stood up and looked at him and had said, "You're right-handed, are you not?"

"You know I am," he had said, his chest growing heavier with each passing second, knowing, this is not good, this is definitely not good.

Paulie had nodded. "I just wanted to make sure." And he said to Carlos, sitting on the other side of the room, "A finger on his left hand, if you please, Carlos. But nothing broken. Understood?"

And Carlos had put down his magazine and had walked across, and in fifteen seconds, Greg had been face down in the couch, sobbing in pain, while Carlos had quietly gone back to his magazine.

Greg shivered again from the memory, looking out the window from his hundreds-of-dollars-per-day cell. He should have listened to Marie. Should never have gone to Mr. Carmichael. Should have never done a lot of things.

He looked out the window, gazed down at the hundreds of tourists walking along the boardwalk. *Are you down there,* he thought. *Are you?*

The door to his room opened. Tony put down his crossword puzzle book. Paulie came in and said, "You're not at your terminal. Is something wrong?"

Greg's throat was dry. "No, nothing wrong. I'm just running a test program, and it should be done in a few minutes. Then I'll be back."

Paulie nodded, made an attempt at what passed for a smile on that face. "Fine. It makes me feel good to see you work."

After the door shut Tony picked up his crossword puzzle book and said, "Kid, them's the best kind of words you can hope for, to make that guy happy. You do that, and everything will be just fine."

"I already know that," he said, suddenly angry. "You don't have to tell me."

"Maybe so," he said. "But I get the feeling every now and then you need a reminder."

He turned and looked out the window again. *Where are you?*

She had never been to Quebec City before and was still amazed that this place even existed, less than a day's drive from home. It was odd enough, crossing over the border and seeing the speed limit signs in kilometers per hour and the billboard signs in French, but when she drove into Quebec City, it was like being transported to an old section of French Europe. The streets were narrow—some even with cobblestones!—the buildings had steep roofs and bright shutters, and there were scores of horse-drawn carriages clop-clopping along the twisty lanes. She felt like they had gone back in time.

She had made the mistake of mentioning this to Clem as she drove around, and he had said, "Yeah, well, history is great but I can't make out this freakin' map. What in hell is a rue, anyway?"

Tonight they were in one of the many hole-in-the-wall restaurants that thrived along the narrow streets, and she was forcing herself to eat. For the past week she hadn't much of an appetite, but she knew she had to force herself to stay fit for what lay ahead. Greg needed her, and he didn't need her faint from hunger or groggy from lack of sleep.

Clem slurped at his wine and said, "I still can't believe this whole mess started over a computer game."

"Not just any game," she said. "The game. How to win horse races, all the time."

He shrugged. "I know a half-dozen guys from where I hang out that could give you good odds on the ponies. And probably cheaper, too."

She hid her impatience by jabbing at her veal with knife and fork. "You still don't get it, do you. After he was laid off from Digital, Greg worked full-time on a computer project that he had been noodling with off and on the past couple of years. He found a way of predicting horse races, seven out of ten times. Consistently."

Clem chewed with his mouth open, swallowed. "So?"

She leaned forward. "Consistently, Clem. Do you understand all the variables that have to be considered in designing a program that can be relied on? There's the weather, track conditions, history of the jockey, history of the horse, the time of day, and about a half-dozen other factors. Greg found a way of tying that all together and making it work. Seven times out of ten."

"So he did. And what happened?"

She grimaced. "We . . . we had a disagreement. I wanted him to just use it quietly every now and then, so we could pay off our bills and start getting a good nest egg. Greg had other ideas. He wanted to go to a relative, a distant cousin of his in the family. Someone with . . . lots of disposable income and a healthy interest in gambling."

Clem grinned. "Connected, right? Somebody in the mob. That's hilarious, you being a cop and all."

"Sure," she said dryly. "Hilarious. You see, Greg wanted a deal. The program in exchange for a set yearly fee, a percentage of the profits."

Clem seemed to almost choke on his steak. "Was he out of his mind? That's the stupidest damn thing I've ever heard of."

She felt defensive towards Greg. "He's very smart, especially about computers and how to make them work. Sometimes he doesn't know people that well. I tried to tell him otherwise but he had his own idea. He went and talked to a distant cousin, a Mister Carmichael, and he made a counteroffer." She paused. "I'm sure you've heard the phrase. An offer he couldn't refuse. If Greg set up the program and got rid of the last-minute bugs and proved it could work, then Mister Carmichael would let him live. That's what Greg told me, a week ago, and I haven't heard from him since."

"So how do you know he's in that chateau up there?"

She put her knife and fork down, suddenly not hungry any more. "A phrase here, a word there. I'll show you later."

Now Carlos was stretched out on his bed, reading a comic book in Spanish. Greg sat before one of the terminals in the room, feeling a bit of comfort in being in front of his machines, in being in his own element. Small comfort indeed, but he would take whatever comforts he could. He went through some screens, checking on a few things, and then glanced over at Carlos. He was intent in his comic book. His lips moved as he read.

Greg went back to the terminal, slapped a few keys. A page of what looked like code appeared, random numbers and letters. Which is what it should look like if Carlos or Tony or Paulie were looking over his shoulders, which was often. But there was something hidden there in the code, thanks to an inspired piece of programming he had figured out in his mind while being smuggled across the border, hands and feet duct-taped together, mouth gagged. There. A message, which was only a message if you read down:

m

a

c

a

r

t

h

u

r

4

4

MacArthur 44. In 1944, what did Douglas MacArthur do? He returned. She was here. She had come for him.

He tried not to let anything get away from him. Time not to hope, time not to gloat. Just send a quick reply, which he did.

Then, as he backed out of the program, the door opened up. Paulie was there, waiting.

"Progress?"

"Some," he said. "Just a bug I have to chase down. Two days, three days max, and then everything will be fine."

"I'm sure," Paulie said, and after he walked out of the door Carlos said something in Spanish and laughed fiercely, and Greg said nothing and looked at the screen, the little boxes of files and numbers, cute little icons that were about to get him killed.

She had insisted on being within walking distance of the

Chateau Frontenac, which meant renting a room in one of the scores of little B&B's and rooming houses in the area. But since it was tourist season and she hadn't made a reservation—hell, getting the time off from the cop shop in Boston and driving here was a chore in and of itself—she had taken what she could. Which meant a fourth-floor room in a little hotel on Rue Genevieve, within view of the Chateau, and which had the distinct advantage of having separate beds. Clem's face had fallen when he had seen the rooming arrangements, but she had no sympathy for him. Good God, what did he expect?

When they had come back from dinner she opened up her laptop and dialed up her on-line service, which luckily had a Canadian subsidiary. Her heart raced a bit with joy when she saw the blinking mailbox icon that meant she had mail. Clem was standing over her shoulder as she typed, and while part of her thought he was trying to scope out the view from her open-neck sweater, he did seem interested in what she was doing.

"What you got there, Marie?" he asked.

"A message from Greg," she said, double-clicking on the icon. "Right after he was kidnapped, he managed to send me messages. Just a few words here and there, but enough to tell me he's alive."

And sure enough, a few words is all she got:

Pillow place half number beast minus four.

Clem said, "What in hell is that? That's not a message. That's crap."

Marie felt herself smiling. "No, that's Greg, and he's being very careful. He must be under some sort of surveillance all the time, so we've been sending each other little riddles and puzzles that only we can know about."

135

Clem said nothing and she looked up at him and said, "Haven't you ever had a girlfriend, Clem? And didn't you have like little sayings or messages that would only mean something to your girlfriend?"

Another of his patented leers. "Most of my messages have been more direct, if you know what I mean."

She frowned up at that little face. "No, I don't know, thankfully. Look." She opened up another computer file, which had a row of one-sentence messages. "Here's what I've gotten from Greg. First message was very direct: 'Bruised but breathing.' That told me he was alive, though maybe not entirely in good shape. So I sent him back another message, saying, 'Loud and clear.' That way, he knew I was reading his messages. Then he wrote back 'Where Montcalm and Wolfe met.' "

"Who?" Clem asked.

"Wolfe and Montcalm. They fought in the Battle of Quebec back in 1759. One of the most decisive military battles in North America, which led to the British conquering all of French America."

He looked suspicious. "And you know this, being a cop?"

She glared at him. "Besides watching the occasional TV game show with Greg, I read a lot. You should try it sometime. Then I sent Greg a reply, that 'Marion Morrison rides.' That's John Wayne's real name, and I wanted to tell him that the cavalry was on its way. And last night he sent me this one: 'QC's Gibraltar.' Winston Churchill once called Quebec City the Gibraltar of North America, and Churchill said that while visiting the Chateau Frontenac."

"And that message," he said, pointing to the latest line. "And what does that mean?"

"Come on, Clem," she said. "What does pillow place mean?"

"His room, right?"

"Right. And did you ever get Bible schooling, anything like that?"

He almost looked embarrassed. "Nope."

"Well, in Revelations, the Number of the Beast is six-six-six. Half of that number is three-three-three, and if you minus four, that equals three-twenty-nine. Greg is in room 329. Now, are you ready to tell me what you've got planned?"

A confident smile. "You bet."

Greg paced around the room, stretching his back muscles. Funny, isn't it. A guest in one of the most luxurious hotels in the world, and trapped. Like a maiden in a castle. And he didn't know what Marie had planned, but he had faith in her. Had to, for what she did in her life. A cop, out on the dark and sometimes mean streets of Boston. She went out to work and there was always that little voice inside of him that said, be nice, this could be the last time you see her. Hah. Now the joke was on him. He went into the bathroom and washed his face and looked up in the mirror. Married to a cop, and knowing all of the macho and swaggering co-workers she encountered every day, he always wondered what she saw in him. He looked at his tired face. Kind of bland, nothing that stands out in the crowd, and definitely balding, like his father and two older brothers. He had talked to her about it, after they had been going out for almost a year, and Marie's answer had been direct. "You're smart. And you make me laugh. That puts you miles ahead of everyone else I know, Greg."

He washed his face again. He knew he should be humiliated at what was going on. Kidnapped and depending on his woman to rescue him. How funny. But in their relationship, it made a kind of odd sense. She depended on him for ideas and thinking things through. He depended on her for her tough, street cop way of looking at things. And damn it, he should have listened to her when he talked about going to Carmichael with this horse racing program. Then he wouldn't be here, wouldn't be dependent on her.

Damn, damn, damn. He dried off his face and went out into the bedroom. Tony was back again, working his crossword puzzle. Still, trapped in here and not being able to do much of anything besides his project, he had learned some things. Like the last names of Tony, Carlos and Paulie. That had taken a little work, but it gave him a small advantage, one he intended to use.

Tony said, "Back to work, brainiac?"

"Yep, that I am," he said, settling back into the chair before the terminal.

"Glad to see it," Tony said. "Hey, do you know the name of the biggest volcano in the Solar System? Two words, seven and four letters apiece."

Olympus Mons, he thought. Aloud he said, "Sorry, can't help you," and went back to work.

Clem, God help us all, was in the bathroom, preparing his demonstration for what he had planned. Clem wasn't her first choice, second or even third choice, but after that desperate phone call from Greg that said he was being taken away, she didn't have many choices to work with. She knew she couldn't do this job by herself, and she needed help. And since this whole adventure was going to be somewhat illegal, she knew she couldn't count on any of her cop friends. So she asked around and Clem's name came up, and after some negotiations, here he was, in her hotel room in Quebec City, ready to do her bidding.

The bathroom door opened up and he came out. "Ta da," he said. "What do you think?"

She stared. He was dressed in a hotel uniform, with dark

pants and green jacket and nametag that said Raoul. "Is that—"

He was smiling with triumph. "Yep. Uniform from that castle place. Got it while you were taking a nap yesterday."

"How in the world did you get it?" she said, still staring. The damn thing even fit him.

He shrugged, trying to be nonchalant. "Hey, people are the same around the world, no matter what language they speak. I went over there and rummaged around in the service areas, and made some guy an offer with that funny-looking money they got, and here it is."

"And what do you intend to do?"

"Thing I first learned, doing some deals when I was younger, is to keep it simple," Clem said. "I get over there tomorrow morning, grab a service cart and knock on the door. Guy answers the door, and then I get to work with these . . . " Clem put his hands into his pants pockets and each hand came out with something different. The left hand had a small Mace canister, while the other one had a small automatic pistol. Marie was horrified.

"What the hell are you going to do with those things?" she asked.

Clem proudly said, "First guy that opens the door, gets sprayed in the face. I kick my way in and wave this baby around—" and he motioned with the small pistol "—and spray anybody else within range. I yell to Greg that it's time to go, we beat our way out of there, down an elevator and out on the street. You're there with the car running and we make tracks. Simple and to the point, right?"

Crazy. Reckless, stupid and insane, she thought. And so stupid, it might just work. She told him that and he grinned like a dog who's proud that he's been housetrained. But there was one more thing she wanted to know.

"The pistol and the mace," Marie said. "Where did you get it?"

He shrugged. "I brought it with me. I hid it in my luggage."

"You did what?" she demanded. "Are you an idiot? They could have searched us at Customs and we wouldn't have even gotten here! How come you didn't tell me you had those weapons with you?"

Now Clem looked hurt.

"You didn't ask me," he said.

Before going to bed that night, Greg checked his stealth e-mail system and saw a message that sent him to bed with a smile for the first time in a week:

Train leaves tomorrow half past waking time.

As a self-professed gear head, Greg was punctual in many aspects of his life, and every morning, he got up at the same time: 7 a.m.

Tomorrow would be no different, except for one thing: He was getting out of here at 7:30.

Driving her rental car, she pulled up by the rear service entrance to the Chateau Frontenac, which was near an underground parking garage. At one side was the small Governor's Park. It was 7:15 in the morning and she wished she smoked, for she needed something to occupy her mind and to pass the time. Clem was in the passenger's seat and looked over, grinning. "Hey, come on, it's gonna be a piece of cake. You'll see."

She tapped her fingers on the steering wheel. "You'll see, Clem. Get in there, will you?" She paused, her voice almost breaking. "And you come back with my husband. Understood?"

He patted her leg, which she allowed. "Get your kissing lips ready, 'cause he'll be right at my side."

He got dressed early and put a floppy disk in his shirt pocket. On the disk was a copy of the horse racing program and a few other gems. He wiped his hands on a bathroom towel and went out to the sitting room of the suite, where Tony and Carlos were watching television. Paulie was reading a day-old Globe and Mail newspaper. On the television was the black-and-white version of "I Love Lucy," and as a dubbed Desi Arnaz said, "Lucy, tu as besion de t'expliquer!", he went to the small kitchenette, pretended to look into the refrigerator.

There was a knock at the door. His head suddenly felt light. Paulie's eyes snapped up and looked over and said, "Greg. Back into your room."

"Hunh?" he said, trying to keep his voice level. "Why?"

Those damn eyes. "Because I said so."

He turned without a word and went into his room. He left the door ajar. He sat on the bed.

Voices. Some voices. He rubbed his moist hands on his pants, and waited.

A louder voice. A thudding sound, and others too quick to identify, and then a loud bang! as the door to the room slammed shut.

He tried to swallow. He couldn't.

The door to his room opened wider. Paulie was there, a wry, deadly smile on his face.

"You can come out now," he said.

She had driven around the park five times, each time

seeing the American flag flying from the U.S. Consulate, at the corner of Rue St. Genevieve and Rue De Classe. She remembered the odd movie or novel, where an American overseas runs to an embassy or a consulate for help. Not in this little action film, she thought, as she rounded yet another corner. The call from Greg had been quite explicit: any outside agencies brought in, any at all, and Greg would be dead. Period.

So, pretty clear. But she was under no illusions. There were no illusions in cop work. She knew that once Greg could prove that he had that program up and running, he would disappear. As simple as that.

And she would not allow that.

There!

Clem was running out of a service door, running across and the street—

Something was wrong, something was wrong, something was wrong.

Clem was by himself, he had a handkerchief to his face, and his face was quite bloody.

When he got out into the suite he was motioned to a chair by Paulie. Greg sat down and Paulie sat across from him, his thin hands folded in his lap. "We had something happen here, something I hope you can clear up," he said, his voice low and even, which Greg recognized as a danger sign, like those red-and-black hurricane warning flags flown at portside when the clouds came and the wind rose.

"Sure," Greg said, not knowing what in hell he was going to do.

"A man came to the door," Paulie said. "He was dressed as a hotel employee, and was definitely not a hotel employee. So he was here for a purpose, obviously. And I think we both know what the purpose is, Greg. So. Why would he be here? Your wife, perhaps?"

He thought furiously for what seemed to be long seconds, and then cleared his throat and said, "Maybe it was Mister Garfonti."

Both Tony and Carlos turned away from the television, and Paulie sat up, taking in a breath. "Why would he be from Garfonti's organization?"

Greg tried to shrug, like he had not a care in the world. "I went to see him before I went to see Mister Carmichael. He said no. Maybe he's changed his mind."

Paulie's eyes narrowed. "How much longer before you're done?"

"Two days," Greg said.

Paulie stood up. "You have one."

When Clem stumbled into the car he was moaning and he said, " 'rive, 'rive, God, it 'urts, it 'urts!"

In the short drive back to the hotel he managed to stem most of the bleeding with a handkerchief and she got him upstairs without seeing any of the other guests or help. He laid out on the bed and she got to work with wet towels and ice from an ice machine, and after a few minutes, he was able to talk more clearly and answer her questions.

"They made me, they flippin' made me the minute I knocked on the door," he said, tears running down his eyes, mixing in with the bloodstains on his skin. "I don't believe the luck . . ."

"What happened?" she said, furious and scared and upset, everything jumbled in as she got another set of towels ready for his face. Lord, what will the maid think . . . "I thought you were going to get to work the moment someone answered the door."

"That's the problem!" he protested. "Two of the guys answered the door, not one. And you know what one of 'em did? He asked me something in French! I don't know any French! And when he asked me again and when I tried to say something is when they popped me, but good . . . God, it hurts . . . "

She looked down at Clem, the man looking pathetic, sobbing into a soiled white towel, wearing a service uniform for a hotel, white socks, and black shoes. What in hell had she been thinking? A joke. This whole thing was a joke. She tossed a clean towel at him and said, "I'm going out."

"To do what?"

"To think," she said, and as she slammed the door behind her, she listened to his groans of pain.

Greg sat before his computer, listlessly tapping on the keyboard. If he ever got out of this . . . well, he wondered what deals he could make with the Big Guy upstairs that would work. The Big Guy was no doubt very busy, and he doubted he'd be too much concerned with one Greg Celluci this evening. No, the only person who cared, the only person he trusted, was Marie, and he knew that she was behind the little rescue mission this morning that had turned into a fiasco.

It seemed like a fist-sized piece of ice was in the middle of his chest. Nope, didn't work, not at all.

And he had one more day.

He looked through his stealth E-mail system. Nothing.

The television was on in the next room, Tony was snoring on the bed, and hundreds of thousands of people were living satisfactory lives outside of these hotel windows, yet never had he felt so alone.

Think, she thought, standing back on the Terrasse

Dufferin. *Think real well or your husband is going to be among the missing, and soon.*

She shivered and rubbed at her arms. Music echoed along the boardwalk and nearby some people were clapping for a group of jugglers. Too many happy people, and she couldn't stand looking at their beaming faces. Instead she looked up at the blank windows of the Chateau Frontenac. A castle, she thought. How true. A castle that she couldn't get into to get her man out. A strange type of fairy tale, a princess rescuing a prince. It would be funny if it weren't so deadly.

So. A castle. How does one get into a castle? A variety of ways, of course. Siege tower, a Trojan horse, a tunnel under the ramparts, set up a blockade, get the catapults ready, everything from history or books that had anything to do with castles, she thought. How to break in, how to gain entrance, how to . . .

Marie froze. She stared up at the windows.

"Fool," she murmured.

The question was wrong. She wasn't trying to get into the castle, she was trying to get someone out . . .

She turned and ran back to the hotel.

Clem stared glumly at the television set as she set up her laptop and furiously started typing, a half-smile tickling at her face.

"What's so funny?" he said, his voice sounding strange since a towel with ice was still pressed against his jaw.

"You want to go home tomorrow?" she asked, staring at the screen.

"That's a stupid question," he said. "Of course I want to go home tomorrow, but what about—"

"Then it's settled," she said, pressing the key that sent her E-mail message out. "And I hope you don't mind sitting in the back, because Greg is going to be riding up front next to me."

And she refused to answer any of Clem's questions for the rest of the night.

Before he went to bed Greg checked his system one more time, and saw the flashing letters that meant he had a mail message. He worked his way through the screens and then sat back.

Impossible. The message made no sense.

He tried to read it from different angles, tried to see if there was another message, but there wasn't. There was just the single, crazy line:

Same time tomorrow, Rapunzel, Rapunzel, let down your hair.

Greg rubbed at his bald forehead. Was she nuts? What hair, what did she—

Then he smiled, looked at his computer, and understood. His reply was quick:

See you there, fairy princess.

The next morning she was back in her rental car, and this time, Clem was in the rear seat, his face swollen and yellow and green with bruises. Their luggage was packed and in the trunk of the car, and she felt something joyous and terrifying racing through her arms and legs as she realized this was it, this was the last chance. Greg had gotten her message last night and on this morning, it would work.

It would have to.

She drove slowly around the park, straining her eyes to look up at the window, to see if there was any movement.

"Almost time," Clem said from the rear seat.

"I know, I know," she said, braking as a couple of tourists, burdened under cameras and suitcases, walked across the narrow, tree-lined street.

"You sure it's gonna work?"

"It's got to," she said, "so it will."

Greg awoke early and went to his computers, on his hands and knees, rummaging around underneath the work desks. The door opened and Paulie poked in his head.

"Problems?" he asked in that quiet, deadly voice.

"Just a power surge problem," he said, lying easily. "I'll have it done in a couple of minutes."

"Good," Paulie said, leaving the room. "Just remember this is your last day."

It sure is, he thought, and as Paulie closed the door Greg got up. He was dressed and that disk was in his pocket, just like yesterday but today was going to be different, thank you, and he went into the small bathroom. He grabbed a can of shaving cream, put it into his pants pocket, and then went out into the suite. Carlos and Tony were not even dressed yet, yawning and wearing terrycloth robes, arguing about what to watch on TV. Paulie was in his shirt and tie, reading a copy of *MacLean's* magazine. None of them paid him any attention as he went into the small kitchen area, opened up the microwave, and put in the shaving cream can.

He closed the door. He was still being ignored.

He went to the refrigerator, grabbed a carton of orange juice, and as he passed the microwave on his way back to his room, he turned it on for a half-hour on the highest possible setting.

★ ★ ★ ★ ★

Clem said in a disbelieving voice, "He's comin' out today because of a fairy tale message? Are you nuts?"

"No, not at all," she said, trying hard to drive without hitting anything while keeping watch on a certain third-floor window. "He knows what I mean."

"But Rapunzel . . . hell, I know what your husband looks like. He's bald!"

"No, he's not!" she said. "His hair's just thinning, that's all . . . But he's got enough hair, don't you worry."

There. Motion at the third floor window. She sped up and parked illegally, heart thumping and car's engine racing.

He opened the window after he had finished his morning task, his hands shaking. Could this be it, after these days of confinement and misery? He looked down at the park and streets and saw a car brake and pull into a no parking zone. It was driven by a woman and there was a man in the back, it could be Marie, but he wasn't sure. He stepped carefully, not wanting to disturb what he had done, wondering if he could go through it, wondering if he could be brave enough to step through that window, brave enough to—

BANG!

And when the shaving cream can exploded in the microwave, he bent down, grabbed a handful of his work, took a deep breath, and jumped out the window.

She got out of the car and was running across the street, when she saw him, and she yelled at Clem, "There he is! Here he comes!"

And it was Greg, and everything was moving so fast and oddly that part of her couldn't even believe it, but there he was, falling down the side of the old chateau, clothes fluttering, his hands holding onto something, something very strange indeed, and then he jerked to a halt, slid some more, and in a few seconds he was there, falling into her arms, her Greg, her husband, her love. She knew people on the sidewalk were yelling and pointing, but she didn't care, didn't care at all.

A quick kiss, that's all she would allow, and when he started talking to her in great gulping breaths she said, "Shut up, Rapunzel, and let's get a move on!"

She ran back across the street again, this time with the joyous and warm feeling of his hand in hers, and she spared a quick glance back at the brick wall and open window and the hair that allowed him to escape: a braided, thick strand of power cords, cable connectors and surge suppressors.

Later they were on a secondary road, preparing for a long drive west and then back over into the border into the U.S., and Marie agreed to let Clem off at the first good-size American city, but she wouldn't let onto Clem where they were going. That was secret, but she was sure she and Greg could make a quiet go of it someplace out West. Someplace quiet, peaceful, and near a couple of horse tracks . . .

Though they had been gone from Quebec City for a while, Clem was still confused and said, "This was a private joke, that saying?"

"Sure," Marie said, driving with only one hand and refusing to let go of Greg with her other. He was sweaty and his clothes were ripped and he had a bunch of bruises and scratches, but he looked wonderful.

"Tell me again, 'cause I don't believe it," he said.

Again, a smile at the memory. "Once Greg was setting up a new computer, and the floor in his office was a mess of cables. He was right in the middle of it, rooting around on his

149

hands and knees, and I teased him that the black cables looked like the color of his hair. And if he ever decided to get a toupee, he should just make one out of his cable collection."

Greg grinned back at her. "And I did that, one Halloween. Made a wig out of cables."

Clem shook his head. "You guys are nuts."

She squeezed his hand. "No, we're married. And we're going far away, and we'll never have anything to do with those thugs, ever again. Right, hon?"

Silence.

She looked over. Greg was trying hard to hide a smile. "Greg . . ." she started, her voice starting to get a bit forced. "Greg, what in hell are you saying?"

"Well," he said, pulling a disk out. "There is one thing I want to do, minute I get to a computer. And soon."

"And what's that?"

"This," he said, holding up the disk. "My program's here, and it works, but I also had some extra room. So I decided to do something for the three guys that were holding me."

"And what's that?"

He winked. "When they get to the border, U.S. Customs will be waiting. And they'll be searched. Including body cavity searches. And I'm sure the border cops will find something to keep them in prison for a long, long time."

Behind them, Clem laughed. "Oh, that's beautiful, that's real beautiful."

She tried not to laugh and failed, squeezing her husband's hand, one more time. "A perfect end to a perfect day, love."

Greg squeezed her back. "Let's see if we can start living happily ever after. Deal?"

"Deal," she said.

My wife and I are fortunate enough to own a small cottage on a lake in northern New Hampshire. Along the shores of this lake are multi-million-dollar homes that dwarf the smaller homes used as weekend getaways or vacation spots. There's always been tension between the yearly residents of the lake and their new rich neighbors, and this story explores what happens when this tension comes out in the open.

Customer's Choice

About ten minutes after Clay Wilson backed his van up the gently curving driveway to the large house on the lake, he knew it was going to be a long and dreary day, due to two things.

The first was when he started unloading his photo gear from the van, and the lady of the house—Chrissy Tate—refused to help him. Oh, he wasn't expecting her to hump in the long, heavy cardboard boxes with the tripods and light gear, but it would have been nice if she had been at the door, opening it up for him while he trooped in and out of the home. Instead, after a quick and bubbly handshake and hello, she had gone back to the long granite counter in the well-lit kitchen, where she sipped a tall glass of orange juice and leafed through a thick Ethan Allan furniture catalog. Even with her back to him, he knew the look. He was invisible, he was hired help, he didn't count. And hired help can wrestle with the front door on their own, thank you very much.

The second was when he got into the wide living room with the floor-to-ceiling windows that boasted a grand view

151

of a thick green lawn that ran down to the lake water's edge. Down on the black-blue waters was a dock that had a moored powerboat and sailboat bobbing in some slight swells, adjacent to a white-shingled boathouse. In the living room the furniture looked like it had been purchased and placed by five-hundred-dollar-an-hour consultants. The flooring was beige carpeting by the entryway and tan tile by the window, where a brass telescope rested. There was a television set the size of a Buick on the far wall, along with a fully-stocked wetbar and shelves that held knickknacks, trophies and photographs, and not a single book.

Then Clay spotted the well-lit artificial Christmas tree near the couch. The dark green tree looked fine, with lots of tinsel and garlands and blinking lights, and around the base was a collection of decorated gifts, complete with ribbons and bows. But it made him stop and take notice, and to know that it was going to be a dreary day.

It was, after all, the second week in June.

Chrissy came over from the kitchen, a big smile on her face, a smile from the customer to the hired help. She had on tight stone-washed jeans, white high-heel shoes and a red, sleeveless pullover blouse that was filled out nicely up top. Her arms were quite tanned and the sunlight captured the fine hairs on the back of her arms.

"I see you've noticed my props," she said, giggling. Her teeth were white and perfect, and her blonde hair hung back in a simple ponytail. It was the simplest thing in the whole damn house, and when Clay stepped in, he started pricing everything that he saw, and knew within ninety seconds there was a million dollars worth of home here, on a couple of million dollars worth of land, and God knows how many gadgets and such. Hell, the damn place had a three-car garage and that boat house by the water was the size of some homes in town.

"You're right, Mrs. Tate, I did notice that," he said, putting down a box of camera gear and accessories. "Is that what you want, a portrait of you and your husband with the Christmas tree in the background?"

She strolled across the living room with the self-confidence of a woman who knows she's being watched and doesn't mind it a bit. She sat down on the couch and picked up a leather-bound volume, and gestured Clay to come over.

"Please, you can call me Chrissy," she said. "And my husband's name is Jack. He's upstairs in his office, working. Even on a Saturday, he's working, checking on his investments, his stocks. Look, this is what we want for your time and trouble."

He sat down next to her, conscious of his own worn sneakers, his old jeans that had been stained time and time again with darkroom chemicals, and his black longsleeve turtleneck shirt. It was a warm day but he kept the sleeves down. He always tried to keep the sleeves down.

Chrissy opened the book wide so that one side of it rested on his lap, and Clay was sure that didn't happen by accident. It was a photo album of sorts, with glassine pages holding in postcards. Actually, he noted, looking closer, they were Christmas cards, the ones that show photos of couples or children or happy homes. He saw Chrissy and a tall man with a thick moustache that he supposed was her husband on one page, and another couple, about the same age, on the other. The other woman had bright red hair and the other man was hefty, a guy who looked like he gained lots of pounds, sitting behind a desk. Dueling Christmas cards, side by side.

She tapped the other couple's photos with a long red fingernail. "This is Blake Emerson, and his wife Terry. Blake and my husband Jack were in the same frat at MIT, and they've been friends ever since. And very competitive friends

153

as well; Blake never lets Jack forget that he was the first to make a million, and that he had the bank and brokerage statements to prove it."

Clay, who had a hard time imagining a hundred thousand dollars, not to mention a million, just nodded. "And the competition never lets up. Ever. Whether it's sailing or riding or running, Jack and Blake have to constantly outdo each other." She laughed, very easily, and Clay wondered if orange juice was all that she had been drinking this morning. "It's even gotten to our Christmas cards. Here, let me show you."

She pointed out the first set of cards. "Here, this is when it was easy. Here they are, with a picture in front of the State House. Here we are, a year later, Jack and me, in front of the White House. Here they are, on a Hawaiian beach. Here we are, in the Swiss Alps. There they are, last year, at a base camp below Mount Everest, if you can believe it. Now that one got Jack plenty steamed, I don't mind telling you."

Clay wondered if there was anything she minded telling him, as he looked over the photos. He had lived in northern New England all of his life and had been to Boston exactly seven times and New York City once. The two couples in the exotic pictures looked rich and content and very happy, and even Clay was surprised at how quickly and deeply he now disliked them.

He looked over at the brightly-lit tree. "I'm sorry, I still don't get it. You want me to take a Christmas card photo, and not a portrait?"

She made a production of closing the photo album shut while the back of her hand brushed his right thigh. "That's right, and we want it to be a . . . um, well, it'll all sound so silly, but we're looking for something . . . unique."

He nodded. He knew what was coming. About ninety-nine point nine percent of his portrait work was straightforward enough. The happy bride and groom, uttering low insults to each other while maintaining their wide smiles for the camera's benefit. The proud mom and dad with the newborn who either puked or howled during the studio time. And the ever-popular family portrait, of trying to line up twenty-three aunts, uncles, cousins, brothers and sisters, some of whom hated to be in the same time zone as their closest blood relatives.

Then there was the other point one-percent of his work. Glamour photography, some called it. Others called it softcore or low-rent porn. Whatever. If this young woman wanted a picture of her and her husband in boots, leather gear and Christmas ornaments in front of an artificial tree for the benefit of their rich friends, so be it. He would still make a pretty good bundle today, and would probably get to see this empty and pretty young thing out of her jeans and tight sleeveless blouse. Maybe it wasn't going to be a dreary day after all.

Then Mrs. Tate surprised him.

"Oh," she said, smiling widely. "I bet you think we wanted something naughty, right? Like me in a nightie and Jack in a jockstrap or something."

"Uh, the thought did occur to me," he said, feeling slightly embarrassed and not enjoying the sensation at all.

She laughed again and quickly touched his leg. "Oh, nothing as plain or droll as that. It's just that I wanted to put Blake and Terry in their place. I had this idea, a theme really, of what to put on our Christmas card. You see, I wanted to print up something that said 'Christmas Was A Killer This Year,' and have a picture of the two of us on the couch. Dead."

"Dead?"

An enthusiastic nod. "Dead, yes. The two of us on the

couch, next to the tree and the gifts, and quite dead." She giggled. "Nice and still and dead. Don't you get it? 'Christmas Was A Killer This Year.' Let's see if they can top that one."

He literally had no idea what to say next, and was saved when there was a clumping sound from the stairs at the far wall, and Mr. Jack Tate came into view. Clay stood up as the other man strode over. He was a few inches taller and had on summer clothes that said he was well-off and enjoying himself mightily: light pink polo shirt, khaki shorts with a thin leather belt, gold watch on one wrist and gold chain on the other, and deck shoes that looked a week old. His face was unlined and tanned, and he had a thick moustache. His black hair was cut short and was sprinkled with gray, and his wife squealed a greeting and stood up and kissed him on the cheek.

"Jack Tate," he said, holding out his hand, and Clay resented an urge to say, oh? I thought you were Raoul, the local gigolo. Clay shook hands and let the other man win the fist clenching, knuckle-popping contest. Jack had a pleased grin, thinking that he had just outsqueezed the photographer, while Clay kept his own grin to himself, knowing that if he wanted to, with an extra squeeze, he could have taken him down to his knees and broken that fine-looking nose with a jab from his elbow.

He put his arm around his wife. "Did Chrissy tell you about her crazy idea?"

"Yes, she did at that."

"Oh, hon," she protested, "it's not a crazy idea."

Oh, yes it is, Clay thought. He spoke up. "Just so I'm straight on this, you want a Christmas card photo showing the two of you, dead, on this couch. In color."

"That's right," Chrissy said. "Will that be a problem?"

Problem. He thought about bringing these two back to reality. He thought about telling them that about a mile or two from this home—hell, mansion!—were families living in house trailers and cottages that could fit in this living room. That these families didn't have to pretend at playing dead, because death was always about, always visiting. Whether from late-night visits from police officers describing a drunken drive home gone bad, an emergency room visit after a chainsaw accident working in the woods, or a funeral home visit because somebody's dad worked with asbestos at the shipyard for twenty years, death was always around. And it wasn't a playful companion.

"No," he said. "It won't be a problem at all. First, what did you have in mind? How exactly did you want to set this up?"

And Jack brought him right down to earth with a sharp look. "Hey, now," he said, lowering his arm from his wife's shoulder. "We're the ones paying you. That's the deal, right? If you can't come up with a good idea or two, then we'll find someone else. Clear?"

Clay held his hands behind his back as he clenched his fists. He knew Jack's type. Lived and played in a world where hammering the other guy meant stealing his money. He wondered how long Jack would last in a world where hammering the other guy literally meant dropping him to the ground and going after his ribs and testicles with heavy work boots. He let out a deep breath, relaxed his hands.

"Clear. I have a couple of ideas already. I didn't know if you had anything particular in mind."

Chrissy smiled, trying to defuse the tension. "No, we'll just follow your lead. Pretend we're your models or something. Okay?"

He nodded. "Sure. Let me set up my gear and we can get started in about ten to fifteen minutes."

Jack dismissed him with a nod and then went into the

kitchen with his wife, and once again, Clay felt like the Invisible Man. He bustled around the wide living room, laying out power cables, setting up light stands and flash shields, opening up his tool box so he would have ready access to the spare bulbs, screwdriver, tiny hammer, duct tape and anything else he needed. While he worked Jack and Chrissy stood by the counter in the kitchen, both of them now drinking from tall glasses. It was muggy and Clay felt sweat running down his back, and he looked enviously at the drinks Jack and Chrissy were holding. Not once did they offer him a drink, and not once did he think of asking. He wouldn't ask. He wouldn't beg.

All while he worked, he heard snippets of conversation from the couple.

He: " . . . want to get this wrapped up so we can get over to the club . . . "

She: " . . . but try to stay away from the Morrisons' daughter, you're just embarrassing her and infuriating me . . . "

He: " . . . if you didn't drink as much as you did . . . "

She: " . . . at least it's done in private, and at least I don't paw teenage girls . . . "

He: " . . . for the last time, I wasn't pawing, her neck hurt and I was . . . "

Clay straightened up, his back aching a bit from bringing in the rest of the gear, and from doing the set-up work. He cleared his throat and Jack and Chrissy looked over. The Invisible Man was now Visible.

"I'm ready to start if you are," he said, and they came in from the kitchen, leaving their drinks behind. The living room now had a 35mm camera on a tripod, and two flash arrangements with reflective screens. Power lines snaked across the floor and for a moment Clay felt good at what he had just done. He probably could have gotten away with half of the equipment and most of the aggravation, but for what he intended to charge these two nitwits when the day was done, he wanted to make sure that they at least felt they got their money's worth.

Jack and Chrissy came out to the living room and Clay went to one of his gear packs, pulled out a Polaroid instant camera. Jack eyed what Clay held in his hand and said, "All this work and you're going to take our picture with that toy?"

Clay tried not to squeeze the camera too hard. "No, this is just what I use for a sample shot. That way I can make sure everything's blocked right and that the scene looks good."

Chrissy said, "Oh, Jack, leave the poor man alone. Look, where do you want us?"

"Sit right on the couch for now, and we'll take it from there."

They both sat down on the couch, the Christmas tree and gifts to the left as Clay watched. He moved the coffee table away so their legs and feet could be visible, and he stepped back and lifted up the camera, and then lowered his arms.

It was all wrong.

Jack said, "What's up now?"

Clay shook his head. "It doesn't work."

"You haven't taken a single picture and already there's something wrong?" he demanded.

"It's your clothes," Clay said.

"And what's the matter with our clothes?"

He took a breath, held it, let it out. "The problem is, you have a Christmas tree and gifts piled up next to you. It's suppose to be Christmas time, but you're both dressed for the summer. I'm sorry, it doesn't work. If you want to make this look realistic, you've got to start with the basics. And the basics are the clothes."

Chrissy said, "What do you suggest?"

"Something a bit more formal, something that suggests it's December. Maybe a dress for you and long pants and a shirt for—"

Jack stood up, face red. "Nice thinking, pal. If you'd have thought of this ten minutes ago, we'd already be that much further along."

Chrissy stood next to her husband, arm quickly around him. "Now, Jack, you know he's right. C'mon, I know exactly what we'll wear. I've got that silly elf costume I wore two winters ago for that club party, and you can get those dreadful suspenders and tie that Aunt Cecile sent you. C'mon, it'll be a scream."

Jack seemed to calm down but he still shook his head as he headed to the stairs. "All right, but let's hurry it up. I still don't want to be late."

When they both went upstairs Clay walked over to the floor-to-ceiling windows that overlooked the lawn and the lake. He let out a breath with a low *whoosh* and leaned forward until his forehead was up against the glass. He was hot and tired and thirsty and felt like rolling up the sleeves on his shirt. He could hear them upstairs, going through dresser drawers and closets. If he had his druthers he'd pack up his gear and get out of here before they came down, but he couldn't. This would be a good paying job when it was wrapped up, and he had worked too hard and long in setting up this legit business to let his good sense get the best of him. *Don't let this one get away from you. Don't.*

Just an hour or so, he thought. *Get through the next hour or so and then we'd be all done.* They'd be at their overpriced club with their overpriced friends, and we'll be back at our apartment, music on the stereo, steaks on the grill, and maybe we can invite up that single mom from downstairs, Melissa. Even if he just rented a video and sat on the couch and made some popcorn, he was sure he'd have more fun and satisfaction tonight than these two.

A woman's voice from the stairs: "Ta, da!"

He turned. Chrissy Tate was there, all smiles and not much else. She had on a red velvet costume with intricate green embroidery that did make her look like an elf, but only a fantasy elf for some adult Santa. It was short on the legs and had a scoop cut up front, and hugged her quite nicely. A red stocking hat with a white pompom on the end topped off her head, and she had on short high-heeled leather boots and black stockings.

"What do you think?" she asked slyly, walking over to him, the heels tap-tapping on the tile floor.

He found his voice. "It looks . . . it looks quite nice."

She dipped, as in a curtsy. It looked like she was carrying two neckties in her left hand. She came closer, lowered her voice. "Tell me, when you're done, when will you have prints ready for us to look at?"

"Five, six days," he said.

She smiled, lowered her voice even more. "Then bring them by Friday next. To the house. Jack . . . he'll be away on business that day. Okay?"

Oh, my, he thought. He just nodded and in a desperate attempt to change the subject, "What's up with the neckties? Your husband couldn't decide?"

She laughed. "Oh, nothing like that. I figured that instead of just laying out on the couch with our eyes closed, that we could pretend to be strangled or something. It'd make it look more realistic."

"It sure would," he said carefully.

Then came the sounds of feet on the stairway and Jack joined them, his face still flushed. Clay looked at him and kept his face neutral. No use pissing off a paying customer.

Jack had on polished black shoes, black trousers, white shirt, and wide and loud suspenders that showed Santa Claus, reindeer, Christmas trees and gift boxes. He also had on a bowtie made from the same pattern.

"All right," he grumbled. "Let's get this over with. I tell you, I'm not doing this again next year, even if Blake and Terry send us a Christmas card with the two of them aboard the goddamn space shuttle."

They sat down and Chrissy looked up at him, handing over the ties. "Why don't you set us up and tell us what to do."

He held the soft silk ties in his hands, looked down at the two of them, his mouth quite dry. He wished he had snuck a drink while they were upstairs. "Okay, if you're going to pretend you're dead, you'll have to do it right. Why don't you both settle in on opposite sides of the couch. All right, like that. Now splay out your legs. You're not sitting up, sitting nice. No, you've got to remember, your body's not moving, it's slack. Um, you're dead. Okay?"

Clay stepped back, looked through the 35 mm camera's viewfinder. Jack was on the right side of the couch, still looking pretty stiff as he laid back, his legs outstretched. His hands were folded in his lap. *That will have to change*, he thought. The man's wife, on the other hand, seemed to be getting into it. Her legs were splayed out wide, showing a lot of black pantyhose, and her arms were stretched out dramatically on the side of the couch, her face looking up at the ceiling, eyes closed.

He went back to the couch and said, "Okay, I'm going to put the neckties around your necks. Tell me when it gets too uncomfortable, all right?"

"Sure, sure," Jack said, his voice grumbling again. Clay went to the rear of the couch and looped the first necktie around Jack's neck and made a simple loop knot. He slowly drew it closed and Jack raised a hand, "Okay, that's fine." Clay stepped forward and adjusted the tie so that it wouldn't block the bowtie.

"Raise your head, just a bit," Clay said. "Now, look up at the ceiling. Good, that looks good."

He then went over to Chrissy, surprised at how his hands were trembling slightly. *Must be getting tired,* he thought. *Plus dehydrated.* He looped the necktie around her slim neck and gently pulled it taut. "Is it too tight?"

A slight giggle. "Not tight enough. Don't worry, I can take it."

He wiped his hands dry on his jeans and then went back to the camera. He bent down and looked through the viewfinder. Out from the lake came the distant rumble of an approaching thunderstorm. The air was now thick, warm and still. He blinked his eyes and looked through the viewfinder again. Jack and Chrissy Tate. Now playing at dead. Must be nice to have the time and money to waste on such things.

Clay picked up the Polaroid camera. "These will just be some test shots, that's all. So please don't move."

The camera felt good in his hands as he moved about the living room, taking about a half-dozen pictures. With each *click-flash-whir,* a square of slowly-developing paper was spewed out and he fanned the pictures across the coffee table. He tried not to think of the increasingly oppressive heat, the dryness of his mouth, or the sweat trickling down his arms and back. He just focused on what was in the tiny viewfinder, trying to get the best picture he could.

After a few minutes he said, "All right, folks. Let's take a look at what we've got."

The Tates got up from the couch and while Chrissy kept the necktie around her slim neck, Jack made a production of tugging his necktie loose. They clustered around the coffee table and Jack said, "It looks fake."

Clay agreed. "That's right. It looks like the two of you are laying on the couch with neckties around your necks."

"What else can we do?" Chrissy asked, a hint of disappointment in her voice.

"Something bloody," Jack murmured, looking down at the photos.

"Excuse me?" Clay asked.

He picked up one of the developed prints, let it fall to the table. "C'mon," Jack said. "If we're going to waste time doing this, the least we can do is to make it right. We can make it bloody. Make it look like we got shot or something."

Chrissy spoke up, her voice no longer disappointed. "See, I told you that you'd get into it, Jack. We can use some fake blood, like food coloring, and those toy guns."

Clay spoke up. "Guns?"

"Yeah, we have a couple of nephews who come up and raise hell every now and then. We have a couple of .38 revolvers that are cap guns but look pretty realistic."

Guns, he thought. *Now we're playing with toy guns. I've got to get this wrapped up and finished. This couple is driving me nuts.*

Aloud he said, "That sounds like a good idea. Do you have an old sheet you could put over the couch?"

"Sure we do," she said, heading to the kitchen. "But first, let me get the red food coloring."

Clay went back to his camera gear and then scooped up the prints, as Chrissy came out of the kitchen and headed to the stairs leading up to the second floor. "I'll be back in a couple of minutes!"

Jack nodded and then stood by the floor-to-ceiling windows, arms folded. Far up the lake the sky was darker and there was the low grumbling of thunder. "Looks like rain," he said.

Clay made himself busy by wiping down one of his camera lenses. Then, he was surprised when the man turned and said, "You feel like a beer or something?"

That was the best thing he had heard all day. "Yeah, a beer would be great."

In a minute they were in the large kitchen and Jack opened the stainless steel door of the refrigerator, which looked like it had enough food to last the summer. He pulled out two Sam Adams and Clay greedily drank almost half of it in one long, delicious swallow. Maybe the day was improving after all. Maybe.

Jack leaned back against the large refrigerator. "You been doing photo work for long?"

"A couple of years."

"Do you like it?"

A shrug. "Most times. Usually it's pretty straightforward stuff. Weddings. Family portraits. Class reunions."

Jack took a swallow of his beer. "I'd guess today's not pretty straightforward, am I right?" And Jack grinned, like he knew exactly what Clay was thinking.

Clay smiled back. The day was definitely improving. And to show his appreciation, he'd boost the final bill another ten percent.

"Yeah, I must admit, seeing a Christmas tree set up in June gave me a start there for a second."

Another wide smile. "That's Chrissy for you. She's a good girl, a guy couldn't ask for anything better. But when she gets her mind set on something, watch out. She really wanted a Christmas card this year to stand out, and I figure to go along. Why the hell not? Makes her happy and keeps her quiet. Jesus, it sure is hot, isn't it? Air conditioning on this floor isn't worth shit."

Then, maybe a bit loopy on the beer and easy conversation, Clay made a mistake, and knew it the minute he did. It was hot, damn it, and he rolled up the sleeves on his black turtleneck shirt.

Jack spotted it instantly. "Man, those are interesting tattoos."

Idiot, he fumed quietly. *Why the hell did you go and do that?*

Clay kept his voice neutral. "One of these days I'll save up enough and have them burned off. They use lasers nowadays."

"Hmmm," Jack said, eyeing his forearms. "Bleeding skulls, daggers, and a rattlesnake. Pretty interesting."

Clay said nothing.

"Friend of mine, he's a cop down in Manchester," Jack said, his voice now inquisitive. "Said tattoos like that, ones that are blue-black and blurry around the edges, you can only get them in one place. Prison."

Clay took a small swig of the beer. "Really?"

Jack nodded. "Unh-hunh. So tell me, did you get those while you were in jail?"

He stared at the man's eyes, seeing a flinty hardness, the inquisition coming right at him. *So,* Jack was no doubt thinking. *Who are you and why are you in my house?*

Clay tried to smile. "Yeah, long time ago. When I was young and dumb."

There, he thought. *That was an easy lie.*

Jack now looked fascinated. "Really? What for?"

Quick, it was now time for lie number two. "Stupid stuff. I got drunk in a bar and some guy was coming onto my girlfriend. I didn't like it and we started fighting. Problem was, I got pretty rough with him and I had a juvenile record for stealing a couple of cars, so I got extra time tagged on. But I did my sentence and I've been clean ever since."

Sure, the voice inside him said. *Clean and uncaught.*

"That's wild," Jack said. "Prison. Man, that must have been something."

"Yeah," Clay agreed. "It was something."

A voice from the living room. "Fellas, come on back, I've got the stuff."

He followed Jack out into the room, where Chrissy had spread a white sheet over the couch. A tube of red food coloring and two toy guns were on the coffee table. The guns were black plastic and did look real. Jack spoke up as he stepped over to his wife. "You want to hear something, something interesting?"

"Sure," his wife said.

Jack gestured to Clay, and Clay wished he had never come here. "Our photographer here. He's actually done prison time. Can you believe that? An ex-con, in our house. Wait 'til I tell the people at the club tonight, who we had in our house."

Chrissy looked at Clay, straight on, and just smiled. It didn't look like the thought bothered her at all. "Was it hard, being in prison?"

He looked away, picked up the food coloring tube. "Yeah, it was hard. Look, I don't want to waste any more of your time. Let's get this going."

Jack and Chrissy sat on the couch, pulling the white sheet taut against the couch. The room was darker, as the storm clouds from the other end of the lake headed in the direction of the house. There was another low rumble of thunder. Clay handed over the toy revolvers, conscious of the bare feeling of having his turtleneck sleeves rolled up.

"Hold the guns in your hand, but limp-like," he said. "Remember, you're dead. Okay, now lean back, let your bodies rest. Lean your heads back, as well."

Chrissy spoke up, her eyes closed. "So, what's it going to

look like? Something like the two of us shooting each other at the same time?"

Jack laughed sharply. "Yeah, you wish," and Clay noticed that his voice was now lightly slurred. That beer back in the kitchen certainly hadn't been his first drink of the day.

"Sure, something like that," Clay said. "I'm going to use the food coloring now."

He picked up the food coloring tube and just looked at the scene for a moment, running possibilities through his mind. Chrissy on the left, Jack on the right. Bodies look okay, toy revolvers are visible. Only thing left to do is to make them look dead. The room lit up, as a flash of lightning struck somewhere out on the lake. The low rumble of the thunder made a couple of the knickknacks on the shelves tremble.

Go on, he thought. *Another half hour and we'll be done, and this bill will be so high, it'll make their eyes pop out.*

"Here's what I'm thinking," he said. "Jack, I'll put some food coloring on your forehead, to make it look like you got shot there. I'll also spray some on the sheet behind you, so that it's more realistic, like the bullet went out the back of your head. Chrissy, I'll try the front of your dress, but it's so dark I'm not sure—"

"My chest," she said, interrupting. "Just below my throat, put some on my skin. I don't mind. I'm not shy."

Another slurred comment from Jack. "Yeah, she sure as hell ain't shy. The Fourth of July pool party, where you took off—"

"Shut up," she said sharply, and Clay noticed how Jack swallowed and his face turned red.

"Okay," he said. "Head and chest wounds."

He did Jack first, dribbling some of the red food coloring on his forehead. With his head leaning back, it looked impressive, though the color was all wrong. Not ruddy enough.

Clay then dipped his finger into the container and snapped some of the food coloring on the sheet, making a spray pattern. *Idiots,* he thought. You'd think they'd wonder how and why he knew so much about wounds.

Now, Chrissy's turn. He noticed the slight smile on her face, the way her neck was quivering. Just below her throat and above the swell of her exposed cleavage, he made two dribbles of the red food coloring on her skin. She seemed startled for a moment at the sensation, and then eased back and smiled wider.

"Guess I'll be ready for a nice long shower when this is over," she murmured.

Clay didn't say anything in reply.

Back at his camera gear, he picked up the Polaroid again for some test shots. Again, the same, reassuring *click-flash-whir.* "How's it going?" she asked.

"In just a minute, I'll show you. But don't get up from the couch. If you decide that they're good enough, I'll switch right over to the 35 millimeter."

He held the pieces of developing paper in his hand, and after they had focused into sharpness, he went over to the couch. "Here you go," he said, handing them to Jack and Chrissy.

Then it went wrong, very quickly.

Jack sat up and exploded, tossing the photos across the floor. "Are you kidding me? Showing us those pieces of crap? They look worse than the other ones! It looks like we're trying to get dressed up for Halloween, never goddamn mind Christmas! It doesn't look real at all!"

"Jack, listen to—" his wife started, her eyes wide and open, but he wouldn't let her speak.

"No, you listen, you stupid witch! You've made us waste half a day, sitting around for this stupid idea of yours, and for what? So this nitwit you found in the phone book, some guy fresh out of prison, can cheat us with a bill when we're through?"

Clay felt his knees begin to tremble with nervous energy. "Mr. Tate, I don't cheat anyone. That's not how I do my business."

He laughed again, face quite red. "Man, I deal every day with guys a hell of a lot sharper than you, minute by minute. I could smell you a mile away. Thought you could razzle-dazzle us with all this photo gear crap, and then get enough cash to buy a boat or some damn thing. Well, it's not going to work! Clean your trash up and get out of my house!"

Chrissy tried again but it was Clay who interrupted. "I have a deal for you."

There. The man looked interested. "You do? What kind of deal?"

The only type you'll understand, he thought. Clay looked around the room. "Here's what I'm offering. I've got another idea of how to make this work. If that happens, and you agree, then I'll charge you just materials. No labor. And if the idea doesn't work, then I'll leave, free and clear, and you won't owe me a thing."

"How long?" Jack demanded.

"Just a few minutes," he said.

Chrissy said, "It sounds reasonable, Jack. You know it does."

Her husband made a show of settling back down on the couch, not quite hiding the triumph in his eyes. "You want it to sound reasonable, so you're not embarrassed. That's why. Okay, photo man. Go ahead. You've got five minutes."

He stepped away from the couch, headed back over to his photo gear. "Five minutes it is," he said. "Just lay back and keep your eyes closed."

Chrissy then said something low and sharp to her husband, and he replied and she said, "Hunh, we'll see about that!"

Clay squatted down on the floor, let his fingers rummage through his toolbox. Another flare of light as the thunderstorm approached. He had tried. Honest he had, from setting up the legit business to going on the straight and narrow, never letting anything get away from him.

But they had pushed and prodded him, right from the moment he had arrived. They had asked him. *Customer's choice*, he thought. *Not my fault.*

There. He found what he was looking for. He stood up.

"Here I come," he said, and as he walked over to them, he held the hunting knife close to his thigh, letting a thumb lovingly and caressingly go over the sharp blade.

I've always been an astronomy and space buff since I can remember (I can still name the original seven Mercury astronauts, and a whole bunch of others) and this story has the basis through the extraordinary good fortune of actually witnessing a space shuttle launch a few years ago. It was one of the most dramatic and awe-inspiring sights I've ever seen.

The Star Thief

Mick Sloan checked the time as he washed his hands in the bathroom sink. Damn. Because of the nonsense of the past several minutes, he'd have to forgo breakfast this morning and he had a busy day planned, a quite busy one, and he could have used a good meal. He glanced up at the bathroom mirror and caught a glimpse of the bathtub behind him, and the foot that was sticking out. The foot had on a black sock and a polished black shoe. When he was done washing his hands and cleaned out the crusty red stains from underneath his fingernails, he quickly went to work, wetting down all of the bathroom towels in cold water and going back over to the tub. The man in the tub had a blue blazer on, red necktie and a hotel nametag that said KENNY. As he draped the towels over the man's body Mick said, "Sorry about that Kenny, but if you hadn't been so damn nosy, we could have avoided all of this."

When he was done he went out into the room and flipped on the air conditioner, as high as possible, and then drew the shades against the early morning Florida sun. With any luck

Kenny hadn't told anyone where he was going these past few minutes, and right now, luck is what he needed. He rubbed at the smooth skin on his jaw as he packed up his few belongings. That's where the problem had started, when he had shaved off his beard and had gotten his hair cut. Kenny had gotten suspicious about him entering the room—since he looked so different from the previous day—and had started asking questions. Mick was never one for answering questions, especially from the guys in the world like Kenny, and when the pushing started Mick pushed right back and escalated, right to a full exchange.

He flipped on the television set for one last look. That had always been his talent, he thought. Other guys would dillydally, think of the different options, think of what was right, and while all that thinking was going on, Mick was getting the job done.

On the television screen was the picture he had been waiting to see, from the NASA Select channel. The space shuttle *Columbia*, on its pad, getting ready for a launch in seven hours.

A lot could happen in seven hours.

He looked down at the open knapsack. Inside was his 9 mm Smith & Wesson, two extra clips, and a U.S. Army Model V anti-personnel hand grenade nestled among his shorts and polo shirts. The hand grenade was a bit of an overkill, but he was never one to go into a situation under armed.

Not just his style. He zippered the knapsack shut and left the room, and hung a DO NOT DISTURB sign on the outside door handle. He looked up at the morning sky. Clear. If he was lucky, the weather would hold, the maid wouldn't come to this room, and he'd get to the Kennedy Space Center with no problems.

He thought of the dead hotel security man in his room. Sure. Luck.

At what age did it start, he thought, when he knew he was different. He wasn't sure but it had to have been when his younger brother started getting older, and when his mother and father had started yapping after him when they saw how successful his brother was becoming. How come you're not more like your brother? He doesn't get into trouble like you, he doesn't get bad grades like you, the teachers don't send notes home about him, yadda yadda yadda.

So what. He didn't particularly like his younger brother, but he didn't particularly dislike him, either. Their house was a small Cape in a forgotten corner of Vermont, and Dad and Mom both worked at the local marble quarry—Dad manhandling the cutting equipment, Mom balancing the books in the company's office. He and his brother shared an upstairs bedroom, with Mom and Dad in the other bedroom. Early on they had come to an agreement over the room—an imaginary line ran down the center and if everyone stayed on their own side, things were fine.

On his side were piles of clothes, magazines about cars and motorcycles and posters of Richard Petty. On his brother's side was a bookshelf and plastic models, carefully put together and painted, made up of jet planes and rockets. There was a single poster on the wall, a big map of the moon.

One night he watched his brother doing his homework on a laptop table he had made from scrap lumber, sitting up in bed, and he was on his own bed, reading a girlie mag he had hidden between a motorcycle magazine. He looked over at the grim expression on his brother's face and said, "What are you working on?"

"Algebra," he said.

"Is it fun?" he said, knowing what the answer would be.

"No, I hate it!" his brother said. "It's all letters and symbols. Numbers I can understand. I can't understand letters in math."

"So why are you doing it?"

He looked up. "Because I have to, that's why."

He laughed. "Kiddo, let me tell you a little secret. That's all crap they slop at you, all the time, in church, in school and at home. You don't have to do a thing you don't want to do, ever."

"You do, if you want to go places."

Another laugh. "The game's rigged, little brother. You think a couple of guys like us are going anywhere? Face it, when we was born here, we were set for life. That's the plan. Grow up and go to high school and marry your local sweetheart, and march into the quarry and cut stone for another generation. That's the plan and I'm having no part of it. All your schoolwork ain't gonna make a difference."

"You have another plan?"

He winked, turned the pages of the magazine. "Sure, and it has nothing to do with them. I'm gonna do what I want, no matter what, and I get what I want. That's it. Simple and to the point."

His brother smiled. "I think I'll stick with algebra."

It was cool enough in the morning air that he didn't have to flip on the air conditioning. He got onto Route A1A in Cocoa Beach and started heading north, up to the Cape. Traffic was light and he went by the T-shirt emporiums, fast food joints, motels, hotels and other stores. On one sign outside of a hotel black letters hung in the morning air, like they were advertising the early bird dinner special. This message said GOOD LUCK COLUMBIA.

Right, he thought. *Luck.*

He followed the curve of the road as it went up the coast, past cube office buildings with names of aerospace companies: Rockwell, Boeing, Lockheed Martin. Beyond the office parks was a long stretch of flat, dusty land, and then a cruise ship terminal, with huge ships moored at docks that looked like skyscrapers tilted on their sides. Up ahead the horizon was a bit muddy but he thought he could make out the gantries and buildings of the Kennedy Space Center. As he drove he kept his speed at a constant fifty-five, even though he was passed on the left and right by other cars and drivers who didn't care as much as he did. His foot flexed impatiently over the accelerator but he kept his cool. No way did he want to stand out, this close to the prize. Which is why when he got into Cocoa Beach, he had gotten his hair cut and had shaved his beard. Didn't want to look like a freak on this morning.

A school bus passed him, and then another. Of course, cutting his hair and shaving his beard had done exactly the opposite—it had gotten him noticed, had gotten him face-to-face with someone who didn't back down, and while he was heading north on this fine Florida highway, back at his hotel room, Kenny was resting in his bathtub. Maybe Kenny wasn't sleeping with the fishes, but it was pretty close.

Route A1A became Route 528, and after a few miles, there was an intersection, for Route 3, and he took a right, heading north. Traffic was getting heavier and the road was four-lane, and he still couldn't believe how flat everything was. The grass was green and the brush and the trees were ugly, with sharp points and odd knobs, and nothing looked particularly attractive. His different business interests had brought him to this state off and on during the past few years, before he started getting tired, but he had never really gotten the feel of the place. Everything seemed too bright, too new, too plastic.

Traffic was thicker as the homes and businesses began thinning out. Taillights flickered as cars and trucks slowed. He looked ahead. There was an American flag flapping in the breeze, next to a full-scale Mercury Redstone rocket, complete with Mercury capsule on top. Two similar set-ups had lofted Shepard and Grissom into space, back in 1961. He couldn't tell from this distance if the rocket was real or just a mock-up. But he was sure of one thing: the sign welcoming him to Gate 2 at the Kennedy Space Center, and the armed guards standing next to the guard shack.

He reached over and unzipped the top flap of the knapsack, and waited.

At some time in their brotherly relationship after a few raucous battles, they had made a vow, never to rat out each other to parents, which is why he never really bothered to hide what he did from his younger sibling. One night, swaying a bit because of his drinking and high on what he had just done, he stood in the dim light of a reading lamp over his bed, emptying his pockets onto the frayed bedspread. Crumpled and grease-stained bills fluttered into a pile, with pictures of Washington, Lincoln, Hamilton and Jackson staring up at him.

There was a noise in the bedroom and he turned. Another light came on and his little brother rolled over, rubbing at his eyes.

"What's up with that?" younger brother asked.

Not that he ever cared what his younger brother thought about him, but still, he felt proud of what he had done. "What's up?" he said, speaking clearly, not wanting the words to slur. "What's up is that I'm working my way to my new career, that's what. See that?" He picked up a fistful of the bills and said, "See? This is what the old man earns in a week, kissing butt and going up to that stinking quarry. Right here, and I earned this in one night, just one night."

Younger brother rubbed at his eyes again. "How did you get all that money?"

He laughed. "How else? Somebody had it and I took it. Nothing more than that. A thief, that's what I am, and a damn good one." Of course, there was more than just being a thief. There was the feeling of going into that gas station, next county over, and seeing the fear in the attendant's face, the fear that made him feel strong, like he counted. The money was just extra. That thrill was what mattered, and he could hardly wait to try it again.

Younger brother shook his head. "That's wrong, and you know it."

"Nope," he said. "What was wrong was being born in this stinking town, and having your whole life laid out for you. You can do what you want, but I'm not following the blueprint. I'm doing my own thing."

"Neither am I," his brother said bravely. "I'm not following the blueprint, either. I'm doing the same thing you are, except I'm not going to jail."

He sat down heavily on the bed, started flattening out the crumpled bills. "Sure," he said. "You're going to college and then to the moon. Make sure you send me some green cheese when you get there."

Younger brother switched off his light. "If whatever prison you're in takes packages, I'll send some along."

For a moment, he thought about going over and pounding the crap out of him—he had learned long ago that putting a pillow over his head muffled his screams such that parents didn't hear a thing—but he was tired and slightly drunk, and he wanted to count his money, his wonderful money, the only thing that counted.

At the gated entrance Mick pulled his hand out of his knapsack, silently saying to himself, "Test number one approaching," and he held up the vehicle pass with the drawing of the shuttle and the mission number on the outside. Shazzam, he thought, as the guard merely waved him on through, and he was in, joining another line of cars, heading north.

I'll be damned, he thought. Maybe we can pull this off after all.

He stayed on the narrow two-lane road, heart thumping, as he realized that with each passing second, he was getting closer and closer to making it all happen. He passed a sign that said SHUTTLE LAUNCH TODAY and he found himself speeding up. Close, it was getting close.

Then the road came to an overpass, and a large sign pointed to the left, saying SPACEPORT USA. He made a left-hand turn and after another couple of minutes of driving, the roadway bordered on each side by low drainage ditches, he saw the Spaceport USA tourist facility on his left. It was a collection of low white buildings, with a full-size space shuttle mock-up front, with another sign at the entrance that said GODSPEED COLUMBIA AND HER CREW.

The parking lots next to the buildings were all named after shuttles, and he didn't particularly care which lot he ended up in. But in the end, he followed orange-vest dressed parking lot attendants, who waved him along. He pulled in his rental car next to a mini-van and then got out, knapsack in hand. He decided to leave the keys in the ignition.

He followed the other people who were streaming into an open doorway that was half-hidden near the Spaceport buildings, the visitors' center for the Kennedy Space Center. It felt odd, being with these friends and family members, for only the special ones were here today, the ones with connections. The early morning sun was quite hot and off to the left was a place called the Rocket Garden, with about a half-dozen rockets, held up by wires and cables, reaching up to the bright Florida sky. He wanted to go over to the garden and poke around, but first things first. There was a little paperwork to take care of.

Inside the office—called Room 2001 by someone with a sense of humor—was a set of counters, with signs overhead depicting lines for visitors and industry representatives. He went to an open space at the counter, and he whispered, "Time for test number two," and as he went up to the woman, he carefully placed his free hand into the knapsack, around the handle of his 9 mm.

"Can I help you?" asked a woman at the counter, and Mick smiled. By God he knew it was a stereotype and cliche and all that, but he loved women from the South. They wore too much makeup, too much jewelry and their clothes were either too tight or cut too short, and he loved it all. This one was a redhead with long painted fingernails and a short yellow dress that exposed an impressive amount of freckled cleavage. Mick wished he had more time to spend with this woman, but wishes wouldn't do much today.

"Yes, you can," he said. "I should be on the visitors' list. Mick Sloan."

"Well, let's see," she said, drawing out her Southern drawl, and Mick couldn't stop grinning, though he did keep his hand on his pistol. Like before, first things first and if things went bad, and getting out of here meant taking this pretty young thing as a hostage, then that's what he'd do. No hard feelings. Just what had to be done.

She looked up at him and smiled. "Very well, Mister Sloan. You're on the list." She passed over a stuffed cardboard folder bordered in orange. "Here's your official press kit for the mission." Then she passed over a small pin that showed a drawing of the shuttle and letters underneath: Launch Guest.

"Make sure you wear this pin at all times, and follow the directions of your guide," she said. "Oh, and here's the mission patch. It must have fallen out of the press kit."

She slid the mission patch over the counter and then stopped, smiling. "Why, look here. One of the astronaut names here is Sloan. Same as yours. A relative?"

Mick picked everything up and kept on smiling. "Yes, you could say that. A relative."

Another night, another job, and his younger brother was complaining something about being woken up every time he got in, and he decided to do something about it. Which he did. A few minutes later younger brother was huddled in his bed, whimpering, and he sat on his own bed, rubbing at his sore knuckles.

He sighed. "Just what in hell is your problem, anyway?"

The face rose up, eyes reddened, cheeks wet. "What do you mean?"

"You know what I mean. You're so big on doing things for yourself, studying hard, spending time at the library. Hey, you do what you do, and I'll do what I do to get along. We both want out of this town. You just leave me be."

"But it's wrong and you know it," younger brother said, stammering.

"Says who? And what makes you so smart anyway? You think you're so cool, so above it all? You're just a whiny little chicken. Hell, you think you're going to the moon, first time you go up in an airplane, you'll wet yourself."

"I will not!"

"Sure you will. You don't have guts for anything, whether it's talking back to the old man or telling the old lady that I pound on you every now and then. Face it, little brother, you don't have what it takes to do anything."

Now he was sitting up in bed, tears still rolling down those chubby cheeks. "Yes, I do so have it, and I'll prove it to you!"

He laughed, started to get undressed for bed. "That'll be the day."

Mick stood among the metal shapes in the rocket garden, waiting. The sun had risen even higher, heating everything up even more. Large birds—pelicans? buzzards? vultures?— hovered around in the humid air. Around him were the shapes and little plaques, marking the rockets and their missions. Scout. Redstone. Titan. Jupiter. All of them now resting and slightly rusting, some held up by cables. A couple of boys went racing through, dodging the shape of the rockets, and he felt like grabbing them by the scruffs of their necks, telling them to be silent in such a holy place. But it probably wouldn't be worth it. The last time he let his temper loose, poor ol' Kenny back at the hotel had paid a pretty steep price.

There was a deep growling noise and then, one after another, as buses rolled up by the sidewalk. He joined the crowds of people lining up and he got on, making sure his lapel button was visible. The other passengers were good-natured but a bit solemn, knowing what they were about to witness: six other human beings—friends and family—strapped to the top of one of the most explosive structures in history, to be violently propelled into a place that could kill you within seconds of being exposed without protection.

He sat alone, which suited him, while other people quietly talked about the weather, about scrub scenarios, about missions in the past and missions for the future. A woman escort stood up at the front of the bus and gave a little talk as they made their way back to the highway. She identified herself as a worker at the Cape, described briefly what she did—something to do with the shuttle processing facility—and she explained some of the ground rules. Stay on the grandstands. No wandering off. Remember your bus number and return to the bus immediately after launch. If there is any kind of emergency—she didn't say *Challenger* but then again, she didn't have to—also return immediately to the bus.

And all while she talked, he kept his knapsack with his weapons, firmly in his lap.

In the bedroom he got dressed, putting on blue jeans, black T-shirt and black leather jacket. His little brother watched him from behind his little desk, where he was making a model of some damn rocket or something.

"Another night out with the boys?" his brother asked.

"Yep," he said, looking in the mirror, combing back his hair. "That it is."

"And what's it tonight? A gas station? A convenience store? Mugging a couple of college kids from Burlington?"

There. Hair looked great. "Oh, whatever opportunity comes our way."

Younger brother put down his model. "I want to come along."

He started laughing, so loud that he put his hand against his mouth, so that his parents downstairs couldn't hear him. His brother glared at him, saying, "I'm serious. Honest to God, I'm serious."

"Oh, please," he said. "What makes you think I'll bring

you along? Hunh? And why do you want to come along anyway?"

His younger brother started putting away some of his modeling tools. "Because I want to prove to myself that I can do it." He rolled his eyes. "I hate to say it, but you were right. I know I can be afraid, really afraid, and if I'm going to learn to fly and get into the air and get into space, then I need to control my fear. I figure if I go along with you and I can do that, then I can really do anything."

He opened the top drawer of his bureau, reached to the back where he always hid a pack of Marlboros behind a couple of pairs of dress socks. "Okay. If you go along, maybe that helps you in your queer little quest. What's in it for me?"

Younger brother's eyes were young but they were sharp. "Because maybe I will get scared, so scared that I cry and maybe even wet myself. You'd like that, wouldn't you?"

Now, that was a point. He turned to his younger brother and said, "Yeah, I would like that. All right. You want in? You're in."

Now he was in the VIP viewing area, set up against the Banana River. To the left was a huge building, a new museum highlighting the Saturn V rocket and the moon missions. Grandstands were set up near a fence adjacent to the riverbank, and three flagpoles were set up. An American flag flapped in the breeze from one and a flag for shuttle *Columbia* hung from the other, and a NASA flag hung on the third. Sweat was trickling down the back of his neck and his arms. Jesus, it was hot, and he wished he had a hat.

Buses in the parking lot behind the grandstands grumbled as their diesel engines remained on, and lines began to form at the stands for souvenirs, ice cream and water. Mick went up to one of the grandstands, slowly climbed to the top.

People were walking up and down the grandstands, taking seats, and some popped up umbrellas to give themselves some shade. Loudspeakers announced that it was T-minus three hours and counting for the mission, and so far, everything was a "go." There were two televisions set up in front of the grandstands, showing the live feed from the NASA channel, but the glare from the morning sun washed out the picture. A digital countdown clock flipped the numerals backwards as the countdown proceeded, and he had never seen time move so slowly.

He sat down, put the knapsack down next to him, put his hand inside to reassuringly touch his weapons. He rummaged around inside for a moment and pulled out a pair of binoculars. Across the river he looked, focusing in, until he saw the gantry complex. Launchpad 39B. Set up against the gantry was the space shuttle, the orange fuel tank bright against the slight haze, flanked by the twin solid rocket boosters and the stubby wings of *Columbia*. His throat tightened at seeing it in person, not watching it on CNN or C-SPAN, and as he thought about who was now inside, waiting for launch, he had to turn away for a moment.

Next to him two young boys sat, accompanied by their parents. While mom and dad fussed over sunscreen, cameras and water, one boy said to the other, "I see it! There's *Columbia*, the shuttle!"

The older brother corrected him. "Nate, the whole thing is the space shuttle. *Columbia* is the orbiter. Remember that, okay? If you want people to think you know something about space, you gotta know the right names. Okay?"

"Okay," he said, and Mick watched as the two brothers quietly began holding hands, as the announcer kept track of the countdown. For a moment he wanted to talk to them, to ask them how it was like, to be two brothers who got along, but this was their day. He didn't want to disturb them.

A convenience store was the target this night, set deep along one of the many rural back roads that connected the small Vermont towns in this part of the county. His buds— Harry and Paul—had put up a fuss when he had brought along his younger brother, but he said, "Hey, this is my night, and I say he goes along. You guys got a problem, you can ride with somebody else."

Considering how well things had gone the past few months, Harry and Paul had grumbled some more and had shut their mouths. Except Paul had said, "You're the weirdo who wants to go to the moon, is that right?"

"Yep," his brother said, and Harry and Paul and even himself had started laughing. He said, "One day maybe the moon, but not tonight. Let's get it on."

He drove by the convenience store, called Liar's Paradise, and saw one car parked on the side. The clerk's, probably. He made a U-turn further up the road and came back, parked on the side. "Harry, Paul, go in and get some stuff. Do a recon, come back and tell us who's there."

" 'Kay," they said, and then they left. It was quiet inside the car, as he sat behind the steering wheel, his younger brother out in the rear seat. Then his brother cleared his throat. "How long, do you think?"

"Just a couple of minutes," he said, his mouth growing dry with excitement, the idea that in a very short while he was going inside to steal something from someone, someone he didn't even know.

His brother cleared his throat again. Nervous, wasn't he. His brother said, "You know, the two of us, we both have a lot in common."

"Yeah," he said, tapping the steering wheel with both

hands. "A set of parents who weren't bright enough to move somewhere with better jobs."

"Maybe so, but there's something else. We both have drive, that's what. We both want to get out of this town. I want to do it legally, you want to do it illegally. Besides that, we're both the same."

"Oh, shut up, will you?" as Harry and Paul came out, laughing. Paul had a beer in his hand and Harry had a small package. They got into the car and Harry said, "Piece of cake. Female clerk, maybe sixteen or seventeen. That's it."

"Great," he said, popping open the glove compartment and pulling out a .38 revolver. "Give me five minutes and then pull up to the front door." After stepping outside he said, "Paul, what the hell do you have there?"

"Something for your brother," Paul said, giggling, tossing over the package of disposable diapers.

More laughter, and then he went into the store. He turned and his brother was right behind him. He wasn't laughing.

Mick took a deep breath as the countdown went into a pre-planned hold. He looked around the crowd, noticed the low conversations, the anxious looks to the gantry and the shuttle, a couple of miles away. It was hard to believe that he was actually looking at it, looking at a spaceship. For that's what it was, no matter how officious you wanted to call it. The damn thing out there was a spaceship, ready to go, and he was about to see the launch.

If everything went well, of course. He looked around the crowd again and began to pick out the faces and such. There. That guy over there, leaning against the fence with the binoculars, who didn't seem to spend too much time looking at the launch site. The guy and the gal over by the souvenir stand, standing there, chatting it up, like they were just there to get some sun and not to see a shuttle launch. And the two guys within a few yards of him on the grandstand, who would casually look his way every few minutes. All of them muscled, all of them too casual, and all seemed to share a handicap, for what appeared to be hearing aids were in all of their ears.

He shifted the knapsack in his lap, made sure his weapons were within easy reach.

"This is shuttle launch control," came a voice over the loudspeaker system that echoed slightly. "The pre-planned hold has been lifted. All systems remain go. The count has resumed at T-minus nine minutes and counting. T-minus nine minutes to today's launch of *Columbia*."

People on and around the grandstand applauded and cheered, and after a few seconds, Mick found himself joining them.

Inside the store it was just like Paul and Harry had described. Long rows of chips, canned goods and other stuff, and coolers for beer and drinks, a restroom door that was closed and a counter with the young girl standing behind. Younger brother seemed to take a deep breath and he stood close, too close, and he said quietly, "Back off, will you? You're crowding me."

His brother went down one of the rows, between chips and soft drinks, and he smiled at the girl. She was in her teens, short red hair, and a bright smile that faded quickly when he pulled the revolver out.

"We'll make this quick and easy, girl, but it's up to you," he said. "Everything in the register. Now."

Immediately she burst into tears, and then she punched open the register drawer and started pulling out bills. "Please—please—" It was like she couldn't finish a sentence. My, how he enjoyed those tears, enjoyed that sense of power going through him, knowing that she would have to do anything and everything he wanted, all because of that hunk of iron in his fist. Without it, he was nothing, but with it, for this girl clerk on this night, he was a god.

"Now, now," he said, waving the revolver for emphasis. "Under the drawer, too, where you keep the extra bills." After another minute she passed the bills over to him, and he extended his fingers, just so he could touch her skin, and then—

"Hey!"

He turned, seeing everything was wrong, everything was wrong, the door to the restroom was open and a large man with a handlebar moustache and one pissed-off expression on his face had his brother in a headlock, and a folding knife to his throat. His brother was gurgling, his face red, and the guy started out, "If you want to see your friend here let loose, then—"

He didn't listen to the rest of the speech. Paul and Harry had pulled up to the door, honked the horn, and he was outside and in the front seat just as they were pulling away. Paul said, "Your brother, man, what's going on—"

And he had said, "Go, damn it! Just get the hell out of here!"

Mick hadn't felt this way in a long time, the sheer energy of the moment, knowing that everybody in this crowd was looking and hoping and praying in one direction, to that gantry and spaceship across on the other side of the river. Before him some people had umbrellas and parasols up against the heavy sun, but as the countdown went below five minutes, they had put them away, so as not to block the view of their neighbors. He was surprised at how damn considerate they were.

"T-minus two minutes and counting for today's launch of *Columbia*," the echoing voice said. "Everything still a go for launch. Launch control has advised *Columbia* crew to close and lock their helmet visors. T-minus one minute and forty-five seconds."

Then one, and then another, and then four or five more people stood up, as if they were in a giant, open-air cathedral, and Mick joined them as well. Beside him the two young boys were straining up, trying to see over the heads in front of them, and then they stood up on the next step of the grandstand. The oldest of the two had a pair of binoculars in his chubby fists, keeping view of the shuttle, while the other one seemed to be saying the "Hail Mary" in a slight whisper.

"T-minus one minute and counting."

Mick hung his knapsack from one shoulder while bringing up the binoculars, trying to focus in on what was going on, but he found to his dismay that his hands were shaking. Everything he had ever done in his life, and now, now his hands couldn't keep still! He let the binoculars drop around his neck on its strap.

"T-minus thirty-one seconds and counting. *Columbia*'s on-board computers now in command as we begin auto-sequence start. T-minus twenty seconds and counting . . . "

And who could have believed, when it all was sorted out, that his brother wouldn't give him up!

No matter the threats, the pleadings, the arguments, younger brother had stayed in juvie detention, not saying a thing, not saying one word. Only once did he have a chance to speak to him, and his brother's words were to the point: "Guess you think I'm brave now, hunh?"

"Jesus, you're an idiot," he said.

"Maybe I am," his younger brother said, his voice calm. "But I'm my own idiot. Maybe I just want to prove that I can do something that scares me so much. Something that I can use later on. Maybe that's why I'm here."

"You think parents and the cops are going to believe you? That you were robbing that store with a couple of guys you met on the street? Why haven't you given me up?"

His younger brother shrugged. "Why haven't you told them?"

"I have!" he said. "I've told them that I was there, but that damn store clerk is too scared to testify. And her dad, the guy with the knife to your throat, he didn't get a good look at me. And that's why you're still here, stupid. Why don't you do the smart thing?"

A secret little smile. "I am doing the smart thing. I'm showing you that I can make it, that I'm brave enough to do anything I want. Even if it's being a thief like you."

Mick found he could not breathe as the countdown went on and on, each second passing feeling like another stone added to his shoulders.

"T-minus ten, nine, eight, we have a go for main engine start . . . we have a main engine start . . . "

The crowd about him went "ooooh" as the bright flare of red and orange blew out from the bottom of the gantry, and then " . . . three, two, one . . . "

An enormous cloud of steam and smoke billowed out as the solid rocket boosters lit off and Mick could hardly hear the PA system as the man said: " . . . liftoff, we have a liftoff of space shuttle *Columbia* as she embarks on a nine-day mission for space science . . . "

It was like a dream, a dream he had seen in his mind's eye, over and over again, as the winged shuttle rose up from the pad, rotating as it headed up into the Florida sky. For a few seconds the ascent was silent, as the sound waves rushed in at a thousand feet per second to the grandstand. Then the noise struck, rising in a crescendo, a thundering, rippling noise that seemed to beat at his chest and face. For the first second or two, the shuttle seemed to climb at an agonizingly slow pace, but then it accelerated, from one heartbeat to a next, rising up and up.

Around him the people were yelling, cheering, clapping. Most had binoculars or cameras or camcorders up against their faces, but Mick was satisfied to watch it roar up into the sky with his own naked eyes, the exhaust moving out behind the bright engine flare of *Columbia* like a pyramid of smoke and steam.

His cheeks were suddenly wet, and he realized he was crying.

For his younger brother, everything that could have gone wrong, went wrong.

His stay at the juvenile detention center was extended, and then extended again, due to his fights with other detainees. He also walked away from a counseling group, and spent three days on the outside before being recaptured.

And when he eventually got home, his eyes seemed tired all the time, like he had seen so very much in such a short time. Younger brother had to sleep with a light on, and he had put up a fuss until his brother said, quietly, "I'll fight you for it. And trust me, I'll whip your ass."

So the light stayed on, and he had a terrible time sleeping, every night, for every time he closed his eyes, he saw that scene, back in the convenience store, where he had abandoned him.

★ ★ ★ ★ ★

In just a very short while, the shuttle had climbed until all he could make out was the base of the orange fuel tank, and the flames coming from the three main engines and the two solid rocket fuel boosters. Then came a pair of bright flares of light and smoke, and another "ooooh" from the crowd. The PA announcer calmly said, "Booster control officer confirms normal separation of the boosters. All systems aboard Columbia are performing well."

More cheers, as the engine noise finally began to fade away. And then another announcement: "Three minutes and five seconds into the flight, Columbia is traveling at 3600 miles per hour and is 79 miles downrange from the Kennedy Space Center and 50 miles in altitude. All systems continue to perform nominally."

He wiped the tears from his cheeks, kept on staring up, his neck beginning to ache, and he knew he would keep on looking as long as possible.

It began to get even worse, his younger brother had put away his books, had gotten hooked up with some friends he made in the juvenile detention center, and his parents began coming down hard on him, the older brother. One night, his father—never one to do much of anything—got drunk and belted him around the living room. "You fool!" he shouted. "What the hell did you do? Hunh? Bad enough that you have to grow up to be such a loser, you had to bring him along for the ride, too? Is that it? Is it?"

So his father had tossed him out of the house, at age seventeen. A year later, after stumbling by on one low-rent job after another, he had joined the military.

By now all he could see was a bright dot of light, as

193

Columbia surged out across the Atlantic. The PA announcer said, "*Columbia* is now 200 miles downrange from the Kennedy Space Center and is 67 miles in altitude. All systems still performing well."

He looked down, just for a moment. Across at the gantry a large cloud of smoke and steam was slowly drifting away. Around him people started going down the viewing stands, laughing and chattering. He looked among the people and smiled, as he saw the two young boys, still holding each other's hand, walk away with their parents.

When he looked up again, the dot of light was gone. *Columbia* and her crew were in orbit.

Years later he had met up with his younger brother. The talk had been strained, for whatever little things they had in common were now gone. They had both gone out of the small Vermont town, and while he had lived at military bases both in the States and Europe, younger brother had gone around the country, doing things he would not explain. Though he had a good idea of what was going on, could tell from the hard look about his brother's eyes.

At their very last meeting, he had paid their bar bill and said, "Please, can I ask you something?"

"Sure," younger brother said. "Go ahead."

He had stared down at a soggy cocktail napkin, afraid of what he was going to say next. "Will you . . . will you forgive me, for what I did, back there?"

His younger brother looked puzzled. "Back where?"

"At the convenience store. When I left you behind . . . I've always felt bad about it, honest. I abandoned you and . . . " He couldn't speak, for his throat felt like it was swelling up so much it could strangle him.

His brother shook his head, picked up a toothpick. "That

was a long time ago. I went in that store on my own free will. Forget it. All right? Just forget it."

But he could never do that.

Mick was now sitting alone on the grandstand seats. All of the other launch guests had streamed back to the buses, which had grumbled away, heading back to the visitors' center. He sat there alone, the knapsack in his lap. He took a deep breath. It had all worked out. He had had his doubts, but it had all worked out.

Then, one man appeared, and then another. Joined by a woman and another man. They all had weapons in their hands and they slowly came up the grandstand, flanking him. He slowly stood up and carefully put his knapsack down, and then kicked it to the ground. He would no longer need it.

"On your knees and turn around, now!" one of the men shouted. He did as he was told, and felt something light begin to stir in his chest. The long run was over. He had finally seen what he was destined to see. Finally.

The handcuffs were almost a comfort around his wrists, and he was helped up from the grandstand. Maybe later he'd tell them about Kenny back at the hotel, but not right now. One of the men leaned into him and said, "The name is Special Agent Blanning. Mick, I've been following your trail for years. For murder and bank jobs and everything in between, across eight states. And you know what? When you said you would give yourself up, just to see a damn shuttle launch in person . . . well, I never would have believed it."

"Well, glad to make you a believer, Agent Blanning. Sometimes you just get tired of running. And could I ask one more favor to close out the day?"

The FBI agent laughed, as they went down the grandstand. "Sure. Why not. You've just made my day."

So he told him, as they led him away, Mick looked back once again at the empty gantry, where all his hopes and dreams had once rested.

So, damn it, this is what it was like! For all those years in the service of his country, in the Air Force, he found an aptitude he never knew existed. He had hit the books while on the government's dime and had actually enjoyed it. The Air Force was also damn short of pilots and he tested out positive for flight training, and from there, he kept on climbing up that ladder, getting higher and higher, from flying regular jets to test piloting to even applying for the astronaut service, can you believe it.

But all the while, as he climbed that ladder, that little weight was on his shoulders, calling him a fraud, calling him a usurper, calling him a thief. And when word came in from the FBI about what his younger brother wanted, well, he thought it would croak any chance of flying into orbit.

But Jesus, here he was, floating in the shuttle flight deck, his stomach doing flip-flops and his face feeling puffy from adjusting to micro-gravity, and out of one of the aft viewing windows, there was Africa, slowly turning beneath him. There were so many things to do, so many tasks to achieve, and still, he could not believe he was here, that he had made it.

Fraud, the tiny voice whispered. *You don't belong here. You stole this. You stole this from your brother.*

"Ah, *Columbia,* Houston," came a voice inside his earpiece.

The mission commander, floating about ten feet away, toggled the communication control switch at his side. "Go ahead, Houston."

"Greg, a bit of early housekeeping here. We've got a message for Tom."

He pressed down his own communication switch. "Houston, this is Tom. Go ahead."

"Tom . . . message is that your package has been safely picked up."

He nodded, knowing now that his brother was now in custody, now faced trial and life in prison, all because of what he agreed with. He had a flash of anger, thinking that this was his brother's revenge, to spoil this mission and whatever career he had with NASA.

"Ah, Tom . . . "

"Go ahead, Houston."

"Another message, as well. Just one word."

His mission commander was staring at him, like he was thinking, what in the world is going on with you and this mission?

"I'm ready, Houston."

The words crackled in his earpiece. "Message follows. Forgiven. That's it, Tom. One word. Forgiven."

"Ah, thanks Houston. Appreciate that."

"Okay. Greg, we're ready for you to adjust the Ku-band antenna and we want to check the cargo bay temperatures . . . "

He turned, pretended to check something in the storage lockers. He knew he would experience many things in this trip to space, from adjusting to the micro-gravity, from assisting in the experiments, to actually seeing how it was to live up here in earth orbit.

But he never thought he'd learn that in space, tears in the eyes have no place to go.

Another one of my favorite stories, this was written for another Marty Greenberg anthology of military stories. The story seemed to write itself, and in re-reading it now, I still get a chill from seeing one individual's name, in the very first paragraph of the story. I wrote this particular person's name eighteen months before the events of September 11, 2001. I guess I had been paying attention to him and his activities long before other people did. Too bad others didn't share my interest . . . including, unfortunately, some in the U.S. government.

The Men on the Wall

The crisis officially began at three a.m. EST at Ft. Meade, Maryland, where a drowsy intercept technician wearing earphones at the National Security Agency was checking a sound file that had been downloaded some hours earlier from a STATOR surveillance satellite. Each day the agency and its intercept stations and satellites across the globe recorded terabytes of information from radio transmissions, cell phones, e-mail, fax signals, and anything else that could be sent through the ether. Each day, only a handful of messages were flagged and reviewed by a technician, usually because of a certain phrase or series of words that warranted additional attention. The keywords for such reviews included phrases such as "Osama bin-Laden" or "truck bomb" or "Hezbollah."

This phrase was different. At this hour the NSA intercept technician—fluent in Russian—listened twice to the intercepted radio transmission before jerking suddenly awake. He listened to it for a third time before reaching up over his desk, where a metal shelf held a series of black covered binders, full of procedures. Each intercepted phrase demanded a certain type of procedure; this one meant going to a dusty binder he had looked through exactly once, during a boring night shift where he had decided to see just how bad things could get.

Pretty bad. His hands were shaking as he found the correct tab and ran through the notification procedure. When he located the correct page, he picked up his telephone—a placard on the instrument said SAFE FOR SECURE CONVERSATIONS—and dialed a four-digit number.

"One-niner-four-six," came the reply, a calm woman's voice.

"Uh," he said, a shaking finger underlining the script he was supposed to follow. "This is on-duty Surveillance Officer twelve. Please repeat your extension."

"One-niner-four-six."

"Right, uh, I mean, check." He took a deep breath, pushed his legs together to prevent them from shaking. "Intercept message Tango Fourteen is a WESTWIND message. Repeat, intercept message Tango Fourteen is a WESTWIND message."

"Understood," the voice said, still calm. "Please log in time and date of this call. Thank you."

The woman hung up. The technician did the same and wiped at his face. He looked over at the digital clock. Less than three hours to go before the end of shift. He went to his shift log, noted time and date as requested, then looked over again at the blood-red numerals on the clock.

There were still less than three hours to go before he could leave. When this shift was done, he was going home and getting Martha and the two young boys, and he was taking a very long and unofficial vacation. His parents had a vacation cabin in the Pocono Mountains, and he and his family were going to stay there for the next month or so.

And if any living thing tried to come to the front door, he would shoot it dead.

In the government there are decisions and then there are decisions.

After the NSA technician flagged the intercept message, it was reviewed again, technically enhanced to make its audio clearer, and then was "sent upstream" as one decision maker after another bumped it to his or her superior. Even in the intelligence community, a decision for some type of action based on such a message could take several days or weeks.

But this was a WESTWIND message. The intelligence community didn't have several days or weeks to make the necessary decision.

Which is why less than four hours after the NSA technician made his phone call to extension 1946, two men were having a meeting in an obscure office in the basement of the Pentagon. At the Pentagon, the closer your office was to the outer ring and the closer your parking space to the main entrance, the higher in most people's eyes you rated. The two men, one an Air Force officer and the other a Navy officer, didn't care about playing that game. They had always had more important things to worry about.

The Air Force officer looked across the shiny and clean desk at his counterpart. "Four days left. You thinking what I'm thinking?"

"Yeah," the Navy officer said. He was going to say something else when there was a knock at the door. The Air Force officer looked automatically at his desk, to ensure no classified materials were out in the open, and then he reached under the desk and pressed a switch. There was a loud buzzing noise as the door's lock was undone. A female Air Force warrant officer came in with a sealed nine-by-twelve envelope, bordered by red and black stripes. She passed it over and he signed for it, and then she left.

When the door was closed, the Air Force officer undid the wax seal and removed a message flimsy. He sighed heavily when he read what was on the paper, and then he wordlessly passed it over to the Navy officer.

"That tears it," the Navy officer said.

"Yep. The Russians have told us that either we take care of the situation, or they will."

"Damn."

The Air Force officer rubbed his hands together. "No choice. We'd do the same if the situation was reversed."

"But it's not reversed!" The man's voice was sharp and angry. "Years after the Cold War is over, we're still cleaning up after their messes, still finding out about all the crap they had done, the things they had planned . . . Sorry. I know, I know, no time for looking back. Not our job. Damn."

"My thoughts exactly," the Air Force officer said. "I'm thinking of using Sinclair for this."

"Sinclair? I thought he was out on medical leave."

"He is, but I think he'll be able to do it. He's down at Key West."

"He'll need help."

The Air Force officer looked at his watch. "I can be down there in three hours. In the meantime, get together a team. The usual, except for one thing."

"What's that?" the Navy officer asked.

His counterpart looked at him coolly. "Domestic status. I'm sure you can figure it out."

The Navy man slowly nodded. "No other choice, is there."

"No other choice," the other man agreed.

When the doorbell to his condo chimed, Sinclair slowly got out of his chair on the third-floor balcony and walked through the open sliding glass doors. His movement was jerky, since he was using a metal cane to lean on, and he looked over the living room as he went through. Original furniture, original decorations, most everything was original. He had been in this place for nearly a year and still didn't have the time or the energy to unpack his belongings, still stuck in a storage facility up on Route One.

He peered through the eyehole, saw who was there. What a world. He opened the door and nodded. A man stood before him, wearing white shorts, a Hawaiian shirt and sunglasses hanging from a cord around his neck. The man carried a small red knapsack on his back. His light brown hair was thinning and his face had fine wrinkles around his eyes and lips, like he had spent a lot of time outdoors, on concrete pavements under a foreign sun.

Sinclair said, "Hello, George. I guess you want to come in, eh?"

George said, "If you don't mind."

Sinclair let his visitor in and shut the door. George went in and sat on the couch, and then opened up his knapsack. On a shiny glass coffee table, George unpacked a small square black bag, and then took out a square instrument, about the size of a deck of cards. He looked at a tiny screen. Sinclair slowly walked over, and sat down across from him, breathing hard from the exertion.

"You're clear," George said. "No electronic surveillance."

"Ain't life grand. What's up?"

George said, "Good. No time to waste talking back and forth. Thing is, we need you."

"The need isn't mutual."

"I'm hoping you'll change your mind after you hear me out."

Sinclair nodded, remembering other times and places, a few involving this man here, before his promotions, before his transfer out of flying status. "All right, I can afford to be polite. Must be pretty bad, to send you down here wearing a shirt so ugly."

George didn't smile. "You're right. It is pretty bad."

"Go on."

"Mind if I borrow your television for a moment?"

"It's yours," Sinclair said.

George got up and switched on the television, and then the VCR unit on top. From his knapsack he produced a tape cassette, and in a minute, the tape was playing. Sinclair got up and sat closer, in another chair, wincing as he sat down. Definitely time for another pain pill.

"Got this downlinked about five minutes before I left to come down here," George said, holding up the remote. "It's surveillance footage from an old Soviet army base, now abandoned. About fifty klicks west of Moscow. Here we go."

Sinclair watched the tape unfold. Little numerals flashed by on the bottom of the screen, but he ignored the numbers and watched the activity. The view was of a muddy field and in the middle of the field, a concrete and brick building. The windows were broken. Parked next to the building was a car, its wheels and sides splattered with mud. The windshield was cracked. Two young men and a woman were standing by the side of the car, talking and laughing. One of the men was heavy-set, with a black goatee, while his male companion had a long, stringy beard. The woman had on a black wool hat and gloves and her hair was long and red. They motioned to each other as one of the men took out a map, and then they walked into the building, forcing their way through a door that was almost hanging off its hinges. While one of the men had a map, the other had a camera in his hands.

George paused the tape. "They were in there for ninety-four minutes. We've edited the tape to save time watching it. And here they are, leaving."

Sinclair could tell that the shadows had moved some when the trio came out from the building, the men holding cartons of papers. He looked again at their faces, at the way they were walking. "Americans," he observed. "College students?"

"The same," George said. "On spring break. You know what I did on my spring break? Went to Florida and tried to get laid. These three went into Russia, trying to document ecological problems in that poor place. All of the problems we have at home, and they have to fly halfway across the world to poke their noses into places where they don't belong."

"Where did you get the surveillance footage?"

"Our own platforms, that's where. One of the last arms control agreements we signed, before Gorbachev got kicked out. We have twenty-four-hour surveillance on the base, stationed on camera poles around the entire perimeter, ensure nothing gets started up there without us knowing about it."

"Real time observation?"

George snorted. "Who's got money for that? Tapes get downloaded and recorded for future analysis. Our big little secret. The Russians could store a half-dozen SS-20's there and we wouldn't know about it without a tip-off."

"Is that how you found this piece of work? A tip-off?"

"Sort of. NSA traffic intercept."

Sinclair now felt the oily feeling of nausea start up in his belly, and wondered if it was his illness or what he was about to learn that was causing the sensation. "George, what's the situation?"

The man kept on looking at the television, but his voice sounded defeated. "It's a WESTWIND. Sorry."

Sinclair grasped his cane. "Jesus Christ and all the saints preserve us . . . Look at the building again. Look at the windows, see how those kids just waltzed in there and waltzed right out. What kind of security was at the base?"

"Typical fencing, except there are holes in the fence where metal's been stolen for scrap. Motion detectors and other sensors, but the base has had its power cut off by the local utility for non-payment. Supposed to be a Guards unit there, except they've been dispatched to help beat the shit out of the Chechnyans again. So the place is empty of security."

By now the tape had nearly ended and George had paused the scene. It showed the three American college students, clustered outside their car again. Three well-fed, well-dressed kids, traipsing around in a universe full of death and destruction, and not even knowing it.

Sinclair felt desperation creep into his voice. "But look at those buildings . . . George, the DoD should have come up with the money to repair those facilities, set up a contract security force . . . "

George now sounded bitter. "Now there's a thought. How come I didn't ever think of that? Hmmm. Now I know. Last five years, there's been a line item in the budget to do just that. Now here's a question for you. Would spending millions in Russia help the president with his wife?"

"No."

"Would it help with his Hollywood pals?"

"No."

"Would it help build his library, once his term is up?"

"No."

George said, "Then you'll know why we've never got the

205

funding. Now let's get back to business. Russians found out a day later that these three kids had been there, and they freaked, understandably. They tried to catch up with them, but by the time they figured where they were, they were in Helsinki. By the time we found out about it, they've been out of Russia for three days. And just this morning, we got quite the unofficial message from our counterparts over there in Moscow. So sorry and all that, but if we don't do something about these three, they will."

"I see," Sinclair said, rubbing at the smooth metal of his cane. "How long do we have?"

"Just under four days. Until three p.m. Thursday."

He sighed. "Okay, four days it is. How confident are we about WESTWIND?"

"Not a hundred percent," George admitted. "But hell, you know we'd have to do something, even if the possibility was only ten percent."

Sinclair looked again at the screen. His voice was quiet. "I've been sick, you know."

"I know. What's the time span the doctors are telling you?"

"A month, two months, and then things will finally be re-solved and I can toss this frigging cane away. Just so you know. And why did you come here for me, anyway?"

"You're the best," George said simply.

"No, I'm not, especially now. C'mon, George, no time for bullshit. Why me?"

George went up and ejected the tape, and the television came back on, showing a music video involving young white men with guns and cans of beer, assaulting a high school cheerleader. George switched the television off and came back to the couch.

"Some years ago, you gave a talk at a seminar up there at

Ft. Benning. About our new world order. About how the military of the future would no longer be involved in major conflicts with their counterparts in a foreign country. You said the United States was like a rich city-state from the Middle Ages, with no enemy in sight."

Sinclair said, "Yeah, I remember that talk. What of it?"

"You said even though the United States was now the sole superpower, that no enemy or combination of enemies could even challenge us, never mind defeat us, that there was still a need for the military. That there would be situations, from terrorists to hostage situations to security matters, that would require a standing force. That like the rich city-state of old, there would always be need for men on the wall, to keep an eye on the surroundings, to be a constant and quiet guardian for the sleeping citizens beneath them. The men on the wall. That was a phrase that stuck with me, that's all. I figured a guy who thought like that could help us out."

Sinclair said nothing, and then got up. He walked to the balcony and George followed him, and Sinclair eased himself back in a chair. Out beyond the building and the docks, the sun was setting. There was music and chants and shouts, and he turned to his right, saw Mallory Square, and the daily worshipfest of the setting sun.

George sat down next to him and said, "What's going on over there?"

"A big party, that's all. Every clear day the sun sets, the tourists and some of the locals get together to check out the scenery. Pretty fun, actually."

George said, "I envy them."

"Me, too. What kind of assets will I have?"

"The full spool. In a couple of hours, we'll have those students identified and located. Your job will be to go in and get them, minimum fuss and muss, and bring them to one of our facilities. But whatever happens, you have to get all three, by three p.m. Thursday. Wherever you are, there'll be assets pre-loaded, from aircraft to ground units. This has highest priority."

"Maybe so, but how big a crew will I have with me?"

George now looked embarrassed. "Time is a problem, plus the circumstances of the WESTWIND scenario."

Sinclair looked out to the harbor. "Go on."

"Two, that's all."

"Oh, come on George, that's just enough to get us in trouble, and not much else."

"There'll be snake eaters, the very best. But we couldn't do any more. Sorry."

Sinclair looked out to Mallory Square again, at the joyous festivities taking place down there. Men and women and children, moving around in the warm air, looking at the jugglers, the singers, the weightlifters. All happy and peaceful and joyful Americans, here at the end of the road, down here at Key West. Less than four days.

He looked over to George. "Just two?" he asked.

"Just two," George said. He glanced at his watch. "I'm sorry, but I only planned for a half-hour visit here, and I'm running right up against the clock. You're in, aren't you?"

He looked down at the festive square, one last time. "Yeah, I'm in."

"Then we should go. Is there anything from here you need?"

Sinclair got up. "No. Let's get to work."

Seven hours later, though tired and still achy in his lower back, Sinclair felt a nervous buzz of energy. He knew where it was coming from: just the sensation of being back in the business, no matter the circumstances. He and his two companions were in a motel room outside of St. Paul, Minnesota. Both looked like hockey players who lifted weights for relaxation, and they were seated around a small round table. Both had on black wrestling sneakers, blue jeans and T-shirts. They had quickly emptied a six-pack of Coors and Sinclair had warned them that this would be their last drink for at least four days.

"This is the situation," Sinclair said, after showing the same videotape that George had shown him seven hours and a lifetime ago. "These three students—Paul Shirer, Greg Wallace and Liz Miller—are members of a group called GlobalEcoSense. They are all students at Colby College in Maine. We don't particularly care what they do or where they go, except in this case late last week. They traveled to an off-limits Russian military base, about fifty kilometers west of Moscow. Supposedly, they were in the area to document places where toxic waste dumps have never been cleaned up. However, while at the base, they left with something they shouldn't have. The Russians have found out about this security breach and have demanded us to secure these three students."

The large man on the left—Holman—whose blonde hair was cut short and who had a thick moustache, said, "Why not tell the Russkies to blow it out their ear?"

Sinclair said, "Because if we don't get these students under wraps in three days, then the Russians said they would. Which means they'll be sending in squads into the country, which means a dirty diplomatic fight and a dump in the polls for this administration. Therefore, we get to do the nasty work."

Holman's companion, named Franklin, nodded. The motel's lights made the dark skin on his shaved head look polished. "Why us? This should be something for normal law enforcement. *Posse comitatus.* We're not supposed to be used for domestic troubles."

"The time factor, for one, and the need to keep it quiet," Sinclair explained. "Look, this should be simple. We'll just scoop up these three kids and you can be back to your respective units by the end of the week."

Holman looked at the man next to him and said, "Here's another question. Why us, indeed? Nothing against you guys here, but best I can figure, Sinclair, you used to be Air Force blue. Am I right?"

Sinclair nodded. Holman went on. "And my man Franklin here, he's a D-boy from the Army."

Sinclair said, "Yes, and you're Navy SEAL. And your question is?"

The Army man shook his head. "We're not identical forces, man, that's the question. We got three guys here, from three different branches. We've got different ways of talking, of working, of dealing with situations. Means a bigger chance of screwing up. How did this get set up this way?"

Sinclair said, "Your skills and background determined what was necessary for this mission. Plus the fact that you volunteered."

"And what's your story?" Holman asked. "Why the cane? You able to get along all right?"

"I've got a back problem, that's why I have a cane," Sinclair said. "And don't be concerned about my abilities."

Franklin spoke up. "Hey, bud, don't worry. It's just picking up three kids. What's the matter, you SEAL guys can't handle college students?"

Holman turned and scowled. "You'll be surprised what we can handle, groundpounder."

"Enough already," Sinclair said. "The first student, Paul Shirer, is visiting his parents, about a mile away. We get him tomorrow, then fly out to Connecticut for the second guy. We take him tomorrow night, the girl the day after, and we've done it with time to spare. Any other questions?"

"Yeah," Franklin said, staring at him. "You sure do look familiar. Haven't I heard you speak or something?"

"No," Sinclair said. "You haven't."

For the first time since George had come to his condo, Sinclair was feeling that this whole fiasco might work out. The directions to the house had been clear and concise, and their communications were perfect. Intel was even better, with a file folder as thick as his thumb with everything they needed to know. They were parked in a suburban development outside of the city of St. Paul in a large van. Franklin had driven to the surveillance spot while Sinclair sat in the passenger seat, and Holman had sat in the rear. Holman had made to drive but Franklin had smiled and gotten behind the wheel before him. "Sorry, Navy boy, this first time out, I ain't sitting in the rear."

Now the sun was coming up, and the outside looked cold and dreary. The lawns were brown and the trees were bare of leaves. It looked like it had been a cold spring. The homes were low-slung ranches, each one the twin of its neighbor. They were focused on one on the corner, painted light blue. Holman laughed and said, "Man, this kid must hate this place so much, to spend his free time over in Russia in that muddy hell. Look at how desolate this 'burb is. Can you imagine what it'll be like when the snows come?"

Franklin kept looking out the windshield. "No, man, I can't. I hate the white stuff."

"Me, too," Holman said. "Grew up in a county home in Nebraska, man, you wouldn't believe the winters we had out there, sometimes—"

211

"Stow it," Sinclair said. "Got movement from the blue ranch. Looks like him."

He picked up a pair of binoculars, looked at the young man coming out of the house, blowing on his hands. He was the heavy-set one, named Shirer. He looked at the pudgy face with the goatee in the binoculars and then compared it to a photo he had in a thick file folder in his lap. The photo was from the boy's Colby ID. It matched. He went into the garage and came out with a bicycle, started heading up the street.

"Looks like our target's trying to lose a few pounds," Franklin observed.

"That's him," he said. "Let's roll. And Holman?"

Holman was still crouched between both seats. "Yeah?"

"Get the bicycle, too," Sinclair said. "We don't want to leave anything behind."

"Don't you worry," Holman said. "In about thirty seconds, it'll look like he got scooped up by aliens."

Sinclair said, "I worry all the time."

Franklin handled the van with confidence and sureness, and he pulled up and eased right on next to the young boy with barely a tap of the brakes. As Franklin swerved in, Holman snapped open the sliding door and even though Sinclair watched every second of what happened, he still couldn't believe how fast the SEAL man moved. It seemed like Sinclair had barely taken a breath before the sliding door was shut and the bicycle had been tossed in the rear of the van, and the boy was on the van floor, holding up his hands in terror, saying, "Hey, man, it's a mistake, okay, whatever it is, it's a mistake."

Holman was straddling his chest, bounding the boy's hands together with plastic wrap. "Sorry, kid, we do a lot of things, but making mistakes ain't one of them."

Sinclair said, "It'll be okay, son. Honest. And be as gentle as possible."

As Holman gagged him with a clean white cloth, he patted the boy on the side of his cheek. "Don't worry. I'll treat 'em like my own flesh and blood."

Franklin laughed. "Man, don't scare the kid."

Sinclair tried to ignore the whimpers and moans from the bound and gagged Shirer from the rear as Franklin drove northeast, scrupulously keeping to the speed limit. This one had gone well, as well as could be expected. They were close to the drop-off point and the only problem came when Holman said, "Sorry, boss, but it looks like the kid just peed himself."

Sinclair sighed. "To be expected."

"Should I clean him up?"

He looked at the clock on the dashboard. "No, we'll be there shortly. Let them take care of it."

Near Stillwater there was a private airfield, and Franklin drove up on an access road to a closed hangar. He pulled the van right up to the hangar doors and as he got near, the doors grumbled open slowly, wide enough for just the van. He drove in and stopped. Parked at the rear of the large hangar were two small jet aircraft, and two other dark blue vans. A line of men were standing there, all in civilian clothes, but Sinclair knew within a moment that they were military, by the way they stood and the way they held themselves. One of the men stepped forward.

"All set?" he asked, his eyes flicking around almost nervously.

"All set," Sinclair said, easing himself out of the van, holding onto the cane, wincing as he stepped onto the concrete. It wasn't time for another pain pill, but damn it, he had to keep this damn throbbing under control if he wanted to get things done.

The man asked, "Where is the subject?"

"In the rear of the van. He's bound and scared, but he's fine."

The man nodded. The other men in the line stared straight ahead.

"Very good," he said. "If you three gentlemen don't mind, we'll take it from here. If you take your gear and get onto the aircraft on the far left, you can be on your way."

Sinclair said, "Sounds good to me."

When Sinclair got back to the van, black duffel bags full of their baggage and gear had been offloaded, and both men were hauling it over to the far jet. Sinclair took a small dispatch case and looked into the van. The kid Shirer was there, eyes wide with fear, cheeks red from crying, and breathing hard through his nose.

Sinclair wanted to say a lot of things. He wanted to apologize. He wanted to say it hadn't been personal. He wanted to say everything would turn out fine.

Instead, he turned and walked over to the jet aircraft, whose engines were beginning to whine into life.

The aircrew had stayed forward in the cockpit, and preheated meals were waiting for all three of them: lobster tails, rice, and salad. After the three of them ate—with Franklin bitching over the lack of beer or wine or anything else good to drink—Sinclair strapped himself down well and dozed some as the jet flew east, heading to Connecticut. He could make out the conversations from Holman and Franklin as they discussed the action in Minnesota, and what might be waiting for them in the Nutmeg State. Maybe they didn't know he could hear them, or maybe they didn't care. In any event, he could make out almost every word they said.

Holman said, "Okay, this has been a weird trip, but already I can dig the food. That's some fine stuff."

"Yeah, I know what you're saying," Franklin said. "I once did a month in a desert north of Basra. Thirty days of MRE's, day and night. By the end of the month, I was ready to kill a camel and eat him raw, that's how bad it was."

"What's a Navy guy like you doing in the desert?"

Franklin laughed. "Doing what has to be done, that's all."

"Speaking of that . . . you got any idea what's going on with this? I mean, picking up college students, that sounds too strange. You got any better idea than this Russkie base story?"

"Nope, not at all," Holman said. "Pretty weird crap but some of the places I've gone to in the service of this country has been weird enough. And that's what we do. Go to strange and exotic places and meet wonderful people . . . "

" . . . and kill them," Franklin added, and they both laughed.

Sinclair woke with a start, realized where he was. In an aircraft. He sighed. Of all the weeks and months and years he had spent in service, how much of that time had been spent up in the air, in government aircraft? He rubbed at the padded armrests of the seat. Though, truth be told, this was one plush piece of machinery. He had been in aircraft that had been built when his parents had been children, and that were designed to fly for another fifty years, and during those flights, a small part of him had been terrified that the wings would fall off or some damn thing. He tried to ignore his lower back pain, looked out the small window. From behind, he could hear Holman and Franklin were still talking, but their voices were lower, like they were trying not to be overheard. Yet the way the aircraft was built, the curved bulkheads easily

215

carried sounds from one end of the cabin to the other.

Franklin said, "I told you, I've seen this guy before. And now I remember where. In a briefing tape my crew saw, last year."

"What kind of tape?"

"Oh, some rah-rah thing about the military and what we do in the world. The men on the wall. That's what he called us. That we were the last line of defense against the forces of chaos. Real inspiring stuff, suppose to make us forget about the cuts in equipment and training."

Holman said, "Did he give a good talk?"

Franklin laughed. "I've heard better."

Sinclair looked out the window, at the lights below on the ground, moving by as the jet raced to Connecticut. Each light representing a town, a village, a city. Filled with civilians living and loving and playing and being safe, oh so safe.

WESTWIND, he thought, still looking at the lights below.

And he thought more of WESTWIND, and imagined all of those lights below, slowly blinking out, one by one.

Holman looked around him, as he drove down the wide street. "Now, this is what I call a 'burb. Man, look at those friggin' mansions."

Same type of van, but definitely a different type of neighborhood, Sinclair thought, as they drove by the large houses in this Connecticut community of Greenwich. Most of the homes had gated entrances to their driveways, and each home looked large enough to comfortably house a football team. This type of neighborhood was definitely an operational disadvantage. Any other neighborhood, a van wouldn't be suspicious. Here, where repairmen and vendors no doubt had to report to the rear, they would stick out like a nudist at a Moral Majority meeting.

Franklin spoke up from the back. "Can you believe growing up in a place like this? Man, the places I lived when I grew up, they were smaller than that garage."

"You really move around that much?" Holman asked.

Franklin grunted. "Yeah, but it wasn't to see the sights. I was a ward of the city of New York. Got dropped off at a hospital entrance as a newborn and everything after that was foster homes, group homes, outreach centers . . . First real place I could call my own was when I joined the Navy."

Sinclair looked out at the target house, a large brick mansion with black, wrought-iron gates, the third time they had driven by this morning. The home of Greg Wallace, college student, ecologist, and trespasser. Less than three days to go. In his lap was another inch-thick file on the boy and the mission. He looked back into the rear of the van, where Franklin sat, a pair of earphones on his head. Since their first pick-up, back in Minnesota, the prep work had been improved. He didn't know the details of how and when it happened, but all he did know was that the house had been wired for sound.

"Anything?" Sinclair asked Franklin. The Navy man shook his head. "Somebody's having something to eat in the kitchen, and I think our target is showering. His sister's in her room, listening to MTV or something like that."

Holman said, "I think maybe we should sit tight somewhere, find a parking lot, until we get better intel. We keep on rolling back and forth like this, we'll get made. The fine rich people will think we're casing their joints, and the local cops get a look inside this van, we're definitely going to be in a world of hurt."

Sinclair nodded. "Good point. Let's go."

In a matter of minutes they were in a small shopping plaza parking lot, next to a commuter train station. Sinclair and Holman moved about in their seats, watching Franklin.

There was only one set of headphones in the van, and Franklin passed on what he was hearing. Before him was a communications console, and he flipped through a number of switches, reporting what was going on in the different rooms back at the target house.

"Okay," Franklin said. "The shower's stopped. Sister's on the phone with someone named Tracy. They're talking about boys or something. I got noises from the boy's room. He just sneezed. Okay, there's drawers being opened up. Sounds like he's getting dressed. A television's on down in the kitchen. Mom's talking to the maid. Or cook. Hard to tell what. Mom's just left the kitchen and the maid has just made an ungracious reference to mom's weight and sexual preferences."

Holman rubbed at his thick moustache and laughed, and Franklin grinned back at him. Sinclair just waited, his back hurting. He moved his legs some, trying to see if shifting his limbs would ease the pain.

It didn't. Franklin went on. "Sis is still on the phone. She's telling Tammy that if all goes well, she's going to jump Frank's bones this weekend. Hey, Sinclair, any chance of us keeping an eye on sis when this is over?"

Sinclair didn't smile. "No."

Franklin didn't seem to mind, and Holman kept grinning. Franklin spoke up, one hand holding gently onto the earphones. "Okay, our boy is downstairs. He's in the kitchen. He's trying to bond with the cook by using his college-class Spanish. The cook is replying in something sweet and light. Boy is poking through a cabinet. Now, the cook is muttering something about the boy's lack of intelligence and grooming skills. Now mom has entered the kitchen. Usual greetings from mom. Son grunts in reply. Mom says, are you listening to me? Son now sneezes."

Holman shook his head. "Christ, another good reason to grow up as an only child."

"Shhh," Franklin murmured. "Okay, mom and son are now sparring over whether son will appear at the Martins' party tonight, and if he does go, will he at least wear a necktie. Son replies that going to the Martin party is a waste of his time. Mom says that it's important for father that son appears at Martins' place. Son says he doesn't feel like going anyplace at all. More blah, blah, blah. Sinclair, should I go on?"

He folded his arms tight against his chest. "No. Just let us know if and when he's going out."

Franklin nodded. Holman started whistling quietly, a tune Sinclair didn't recognize. Franklin reached over to the communications console, adjusted a knob. His voice was low, no more tone of humor in it. "Okay. Movement. Mom is still yapping about the Martins' dinner party. Son Greg makes comment about Martin owning dad's balls because of all the stock options he controls. More yapping from mom. Sounds like son's getting a coat on. Okay, he's telling mom he's gotta go for a walk, clear his head. Sounds like this might be it, boss."

Sinclair looked out at the crowded parking lot, as the commuters walked and hurried to the outbound trains. He imagined what it might be like, what it would look like, if these cars were still here, unmoving, decades later. The paint would fade and the tires would slowly flatten, but the windows would probably remain intact. Yeah, they probably would.

"Let's go," he said.

The pickup was even easier than the first one, for there was no bicycle to worry about. They returned to the neighborhood and there he was, tall and with a stringy beard, strolling along the sidewalk, hands in pockets, long scarf trailing behind his Army surplus coat. "Look at that," Holman said, driving the van. "Kid's got more money than he knows what to do with, and he dresses like he goes dumpster diving every day."

"Basics of economics for students," Franklin said, crouched in the rear of the van. "Those who don't have money try to look their best. Those who do have money try to look their worst."

Sinclair said, "All right, get ready."

Holman pulled ahead of the strolling college student, and then pulled the van sharply to the right. Again, the door rattled open and Franklin leapt out, and almost as quickly, came back in with the struggling and shouting college student. Even before the door slid shut, Holman had accelerated the van and they were heading out of the neighborhood. Franklin moved quickly and just as before, the young man was bound and gagged on the floor of the van. Sinclair looked behind and said, "Keep him comfortable, all right? Make sure he can breath. Tell him everything will be all right."

Franklin did just that, and Sinclair turned back in his seat, leaned his head against the passenger window. There. Two down, just one to go. They were heading to another commuter airport for the drop-off, only about ten minutes away. Then, up to Maine with time to spare and then this job would be done, and he could head back south, to rest his cold bones in the bright sun of Key West. There, the drinks were plentiful and the women so beautiful to look at . . .

"Boss," Holman said, his voice tight. "We've got a cruiser coming up behind us like it's got a rocket up its ass."

Sinclair opened his eyes, glanced at the sideview mirror. A white police cruiser with a solitary officer inside. Damn. He swiveled in the seat and said to Franklin, "Get ready, all right?"

Franklin looked grim but went to work, opening up a black zippered duffel bag. On the van floor Greg Wallace started grunting behind his gag and Franklin tapped him on the side of his head. "Shut up, will you?"

Holman said, "What next?"

His chest felt constricted. What has to be done, that's going to be what's next. What has to be done. Sinclair said, "Holman, the moment he switches on his lights, pull over. Then tell us when he's stopped. Franklin, when you get the word the cruiser's stopped, pop open the rear and disable the cruiser. All right? But try not to injure the officer."

"Try?" Franklin asked skeptically.

WESTWIND, he thought. "Yeah, try."

Holman called out, "Blue lights are on. I guess that neighborhood back there pays attention to strangers. Damn nosy people."

Sinclair said, "Stop yapping and pull over, all right?"

His back spasmed in another bolt of pain, as Holman switched on the directional and the van pulled over to the right. Franklin clambered to the rear of the van, an HK MP-5 submachine gun in his hands and then, everything went loud and quick. Holman kept the van in drive, the engine running, and called out, "He's stopped." Franklin seemed to take a deep breath as he worked the action of his weapon, and then both rear doors blew open as he popped the latch and kicked his feet out.

Even though he was expecting it, Sinclair ducked and flinched as the stuttering roar of the MP-5 pounded through the van and Sinclair barely noted the parked cruiser behind them. There was movement as the cop ducked behind the dashboard and the windshield blew in, as Franklin sprayed back and forth, the hood of the car being chewed up, the cruiser seeming to collapse in front as both tires were blown out.

"Go, go, go!" Sinclair yelled, and Franklin fell back, closing the doors, the smell of burnt powder overwhelming, empty brass cartridges rolling around the van floor, the college student screaming dully behind the tape across his mouth.

Holman pulled out and accelerated, and Sinclair felt pushed against the seat. Franklin cursed and said, "Somebody better be good at clean-up, or we'll all be going to the big house."

Holman spoke up and Sinclair interrupted. "Franklin. Get on the horn with our airport contact." He flipped through the file folder on his lap. "The contact name is VIKING. Tell them what just happened. Tell them to be ready. We'll be there shortly."

Franklin said, "Should we tell them to have a bail bondsman ready, too?"

Sinclair said nothing. Holman laughed from behind the driver's wheel. And the center of all their attention, the college student named Greg Wallace, kept on moaning and struggling against his bonds.

At the airport this time, they moved quickly, driving into another hangar. No time for talking, no time for a formal turnover, Sinclair moved them along, grabbing their gear, their duffel bags, heading to another small jet aircraft. The jet was moving out of the hangar before the door was fully closed, and they were still buckling into the seats when the aircraft clawed its way up into the frigid air.

"Look down there," Franklin said. "Man, I haven't seen so many cop cars in all my life."

Sinclair spared a glance out the window as the jet circled over the airport. A long line of cruisers were converging on the hangar, just as another jet raced out. The one carrying the transfer squad and the college student. Sinclair clenched his fists, watching the jet go down the runway. A couple of cruisers gave chase, but it wasn't even close. The jet made its way up and Sinclair let his hands relax. There. Both in the air. On the ground, there were problems of questions and detention and overnight arrests, but here, in the air, they were relatively safe.

The flight to Maine was under an hour, and dinner was steak and potatoes and salad, and again, no booze. Franklin shook his head as he ate. "Man," he repeated at least three times. "A black man with a machine gun, trying to kill a white cop in a Connecticut suburb. If I'd been caught, they'd have put me in prison for a century, at least."

Holman said, "The training the taxpayers paid for, you'd just stage a breakout."

Franklin cleaned his plate with a piece of hard roll. "Staging a breakout is no problem. Living through one is another thing entirely. Hey, Sinclair."

His stomach seemed to accept the dinner with no problem. A small victory. Sinclair said, "Yes?"

"Just what in hell is going on here, anyway?" Franklin asked.

Sinclair stared at him with a steady gaze. "What do you mean?"

Holman spoke up. "What my bud means is this. All this muscle, all this firepower, m'man Franklin here blasting away a civilian cop car, all of this over three simple college students. It don't make sense, Russkies or no Russkies. I mean, why in hell are we doing this?"

"Because we were ordered to, and because you earlier volunteered to take on special domestic assignments. That's why we're doing this."

Franklin looked over at Holman. "Sorry, boss. You're gonna need to do better than that. Tell us again, why are the Russkies so hot on getting those three?"

"They're trespassers, that's why."

Holman shook his head. "No, you said something earlier. The first time we met. You said those three left with something they shouldn't have. And what might that be?"

Sinclair looked at both men, both strong and smart and tough, both of whom could kill him in a half-dozen or so different ways if they so desired. He took a breath, felt the tug at his lower back. "All right. Three words. Three words to explain what those kids did in Russia. Okay?"

He leaned over closer to the Navy man and the Army man. "Okay. Three words. Need to know. All right? You got a problem with anything on this little job, remember those three words. Need to know. And right now, you two don't have it. What you do have are legitimate orders from superior officers to perform this action, and I sincerely hope you don't have any problems with that. Do I make myself clear?"

There was a pause as the jet continued winging its way to Maine. A small bump of turbulence. Holman and Franklin looked at each other.

"Perfectly clear," Holman said.

"Perfectly clear," Franklin said.

"Good," Sinclair said.

They were in Maine, about an hour's drive to the last target house, the one where Liz Miller lived. Their rented van—again, stuffed full with comm gear, equipment and duffel bags—was parked outside of the Honeydew Motel. He was laying down on top of his bed, his back still throbbing even though he had taken a pain pill almost a half hour earlier. Jesus, was his body beginning to get used to the drugs?

Sinclair had the television on but had muted the sound, so when the president came on, performing some idiot Rose Garden ceremony, he picked up the phone and dialed a number from memory. When it was finally answered after three different transfers, he sighed and said, "George?"

"Yeah," came the tired voice in reply. "That was one hell of a foul-up up there in Connecticut."

"So I noticed. You managing to keep the fires under control?"

"It's a stretch, but yeah, we are. What do you have planned for tomorrow? Kidnap the governor of Maine?"

On the television the president's wife was holding a press conference of her own in New York City. "Only if he gets in the way. How are our friends overseas doing?"

"The boys from the Kremlin are happy with the progress so far. They just want to make sure everything's wrapped up by three tomorrow. Can we assure them of that?"

"We surely can," Sinclair said.

"Good," George said. "Latest intel is that there's at least one, and maybe two, Russian squads in-country. I think they'll be shadowing you tomorrow, make sure you get the job done. So make sure you get it done right."

On the television the Speaker of the House was holding a press conference on the steps of the Capitol. He switched the television off.

"We'll do it right, don't worry."

"Remember, she has to be with the transfer crew at three p.m. Or . . . "

"I know. Three p.m."

He hung up the phone, rubbed at his temples. Three p.m. WESTWIND. And he imagined a time when one turned on the television, and every station was blank with static.

★ ★ ★ ★ ★

In the morning, after breakfast in the motel coffee shop, they went to their van. It was Franklin's turn to drive and when he climbed into the front seat, Sinclair checked his watch. It was nine a.m. They had six hours before the deadline. And the target was only an hour away, and the airport for the transfer was fifteen minutes from the target's home.

Time, plenty of time.

Franklin turned the key. Nothing happened, except a little click sounded out. Sinclair glanced over. "Tell me you're playing a little game," Sinclair said, his voice tight. "Tell me you're just fooling around."

Franklin turned the key. Click. "Sorry, boss. No joking from me. Damn thing won't start."

Holman said from the rear, "Sounds like the battery croaked out on us."

"It ran fine yesterday," Franklin said.

"Man, look at all the electrical gear we've got back here. Something not wired right, something left on overnight, anything like that could have drained the battery."

Sinclair grasped his cane tight. "I don't care if the battery fairy came in and took the damn thing, we've got to get going. Holman, get to the motel. Start working the phones. Start working now. There's got to be a garage around here. And there's no time to waste."

He looked at his watch. Ten minutes past nine.

It took Franklin another ten minutes to locate a garage nearby. It took more than a half-hour for the wrecker to find their van. Once the wrecker arrived, the teenage boy driving the greasy rig apologized when he realized that he had forgotten a set of jumper cables back at the service station.

All while the minutes passed, Sinclair kept on holding

onto his cane, tighter and tighter, even ignoring the increasing throbbing in his back.

When the van roared into life and started on its way, it was nearly 11 a.m.

Sinclair kept quiet, and Holman and Franklin, sensing his mood, said not a word, all the way to the town of Landru.

The house Liz Miller lived in was a rambling white farmhouse, on top of a hill. A muddy driveway led up to the house, and they were parked on the side of the country lane. It was poorly-paved and bumpy and the potholes felt like they had been repaired with broken pottery. Along the way, Franklin misread the map and that had added a half-hour to the trip. Sinclair was surprised at how he was able to keep everything under control. What was another thirty minutes or so, so long as the job got done by three p.m.?

Holman had the earphones on this time, and he shook his head in disgust. "I don't know boss, what I'm picking up is filled with static and popping. Maybe the sound guys didn't do a good job."

Franklin spoke up, "Well, there's a power line going through the back meadow. Might be getting interference."

"Never mind that," Sinclair said. "What do you have?"

"A couple of female voices that keep on cutting in and cutting out," the Navy man said, delicately adjusting a dial. "One's older and the other's younger. It seems like one of them has a cold or something, but I can't make it out. Damn it, boss, why don't we just go in an scoop her up?"

"And suppose dad's in there, taking a nap with a shotgun under the bed?" Sinclair asked, looking up at the farmhouse. "No, we had our chance at fame in the newspapers with Connecticut yesterday. We can't pull the same stunt twice. We'll wait."

"But the deadline," Franklin said. "We've got to get her picked up and with the transfer crew by three p.m."

He looked at the dashboard clock. It was just past one p.m. Sinclair sighed. Of all the jobs and duties he had performed, to end up here at a muddy farmhouse in rural Maine. A hell of a thing to put on one's tombstone. "We wait another half hour and then we get her out on a pretext. A phone call or something. Anything to get her out of the house and—"

Holman interrupted. "We've got movement. Sounds like she's going out to the drugstore. Hold on, yep, door is opening."

From his lap Sinclair picked up a pair of binoculars, looked up at the house. A woman in a long coat bundled about her strolled out of the house and into a dark green pickup truck. Even at this distance, he could make out her long, red hair. "Movement is correct," Sinclair said, heart thumping, thinking, just a few minutes more. "Franklin, let her pass us as she heads into town, and then get right up behind her. If the road stays clear, we'll take her."

Franklin started up the engine, and the sound of the loud engine was reassuring. "Take her and be done, that sounds so fine."

But still, it wouldn't be easy. As they followed the pickup truck into the small town of Landru, it seemed every time the road emptied another car or truck would appear. Holman cursed and tugged away the earphones. "Crappy equipment, boss, I'm sorry. All I'm getting now is static."

Sinclair looked ahead, still making out the red hair of the target through the rear window of the pickup truck. "Don't worry about it, we'll be fine."

Eventually the number of homes began to increase, and then they came to an intersection with a stoplight. The pickup truck made a right-hand turn and then made a left, into a small plaza that had a bank, a video rental store, a laundromat and a drugstore. Sinclair thumped his cane against the floor of the van a couple of times.

"Okay," he said, as Franklin pulled into the parking lot. "We let her get into the drugstore, and then we get her as she leaves. Holman, work your magic or something, but convince her to come over to the van. Time's getting tight."

"Sure," Holman said. "I'll tell her that I have a sick puppy in the van. Something like that always works with college girls."

Franklin shook his head. "Man, spare me."

"Shut up," Sinclair said. "She's stopping."

Which was true. The dark green pickup truck with Maine license plates and a peeling THINK LOCALLY ACT GLOBALLY bumper sticker came to a stop near the drugstore. Sinclair couldn't move his eyes, staring at the truck. It seemed like a long time had passed while the woman inside went through the glove compartment, and then examined something in her purse.

"I think she's filling out a deposit slip or something for the bank," Franklin said. "Maybe getting two errands down at once."

"There's a thought," Holman said.

Quiet, Sinclair thought. *All of you, just please shut up.*

And then the door opened up and she stepped out, red hair in the light, just like the Colby photo he had in his lap, with the intel file, and he looked at the smiling woman as she strolled into the drugstore and looked at the photo and looked at her and looked at the photo and—

"Franklin, turn this damn thing around and get back to the house! That's not her, that's her damn mother!"

229

He backed up the van and Sinclair continued, saying, "Keep it slow, keep it real, we don't have time to get stopped by the cops, and we don't have any time for fancy, all right? No time for fancy."

In the end, it turned out not to be fancy at all. Franklin raced the van up the driveway and then put the van in park, engine running, and he and Holman just went up to the porch and burst in. There were some yells and screaming that Sinclair could make out, and then the two of them reemerged, the young girl struggling in their grasp, a blue down comforter wrapped around her. They get her secured in the rear of the van and just as they got back on the road, heading to the airport, a dark green pickup truck with a red-haired mother passed them, heading back to a place that would no longer be called a home.

Sinclair kept his eyes closed, listening to the girl moan and struggle, and then he only opened them up when Holman said quietly, "Boss, I think she's sick. She's got a fever. Maybe I should get the gag off before she vomits and chokes."

"That's a good idea," Sinclair said.

Some minutes later Franklin made a point of sighing in relief as they reached the airport gate. "Hey, we're here. We're finally here. Not bad, eh?"

Sinclair looked at the clock, feeling everything inside his chest just slow down and turn cold. It was quarter-past three in the afternoon.

"No, not bad at all," he said. "Franklin, pull up to the rear of the hangar. All right? Holman, get on the horn to the transfer crew. Just tell them one thing, all right. MONK. That's the word. MONK."

"This last one, it's going to be different?" Holman asked.

"Just make the damn call, all right?" Sinclair said, trying to hold his temper in check.

"Okay, okay, boss. Call will be made."

As they waited behind the hangar, the engine running, listening to a radio station out of Portland and the college girl's coughing, Franklin said, "We got movement over here, boss. Another van."

"What's it doing?"

"It's just sitting there, looking at us."

Sinclair looked over. The hangar was at the end of the long runway, and at the rear there were storage tanks, dumpsters, and rusting heaps of equipment. A white van was parked, its engine also running. "Who's in the van?" Holman asked, peering over their shoulders through the windshield.

Franklin said, "A couple of white guys, that's all. You think they're cops or something?"

Despite everything, Sinclair smiled. "Give them a wave, boys. They're your counterparts, from Mother Russia. Just making sure everything's happening as planned."

"Frig them," Holman muttered. "And I still want to know why—"

Franklin spoke up, his voice filled with awe. "Will you look at that? Are they actually going to land here? Jesus, the runway must be only—"

The sound of the low-flying jet drowned them out, as the Air Force C-141 made a low swoop across the field, and then rose up for a long, banking curve. Holman said, "That's our pickup? A jet transport? Man, why don't they just invite the local TV station to film us?"

The other van drove away. The college girl started coughing. Ever since the gag came off, she had not said a word. Poor girl. Sinclair said, "Once the Starlifter's on the

231

ground, Franklin, drive right up the cargo ramp. All right?"

Franklin said, "Okay, but only if the damn thing lands in one piece. I can't see how they're going to make it."

The coughing grew louder. Sinclair said, "It'll make it, don't you worry."

There were people clustered around the small airport building, standing there with their mouths agape, as they sped across the runway to the open cargo ramp of the Air Force jet. He wondered what they were thinking and pushed it away. Just a few minutes more and everything would be done. Everything.

Franklin slowed the van and then drove up the ramp, switching on his headlights. A piece of equipment clattered to the floor as the van canted back at a sharp angle. When they were inside the aircraft, the ramp began slowly closing behind them.

"The crew," Holman said, "where's the crew?"

"Engine off and in park, all right?"

"Sure, boss," Franklin said. "Oh my . . . "

Up forward was a temporary bulkhead, bulging, that looked like it was made out of thick rubber. A zipper in the center opened up and three men emerged from the bulkhead, each one of them wearing white decontamination suits, with airpack and clear bubble helmet. All of them had thick black gloves on their hands, and they quickly and efficiently secured the van to the aircraft's floor with straps and turnbuckles.

When they were done and went back into the bulkhead, Sinclair winced as the cold barrel of a weapon was pressed against his ear. "You talk to us, and you talk to us now," Holman said, his voice filled with fury. "Or I'll splatter your brains against the windshield. Me and Franklin, we sure as hell now have a need to know."

Sinclair slowly nodded his head. "You certainly do."

In the Pentagon, the Air Force officer named George talked to his Navy counterpart.

"Mission accomplished," George said.

The Navy man exhaled loudly. "Thank God."

"But we took a hit," he said. "A big one."

"Go on," the Navy man said. "Tell me more."

And so he did.

Sinclair kept his hands clear, not knowing how Holman would react, but Franklin beat him to it. "Those college students," he said, arms draped over the now useless steering wheel. "They got exposed to something out there in Russia, didn't they?"

"Yes, they did. That was a biowarfare laboratory they were in. It was suppose to be deactivated, safe and secure. But it wasn't."

"Three strikes and you're out," Franklin muttered.

"What is it?" Holman demanded, the pistol still in his hands. "What the hell is it? Is there a treatment, a cure?"

Sinclair looked out the windshield, at the brightly-lit interior of the aircraft. He almost chuckled. No matter how you cut it, this was probably his last flight in a government-owned jet, heading to a secure medical facility in Nevada. God bless America.

"Be real," Sinclair said. "That laboratory was for biowarfare. It wasn't for medical research. All we've been told is that after exposure, there's a seven-day dormant phase. After the seven days, the person who's been exposed becomes quite ill and quite contagious."

The coughing grew louder. "The deadline," Franklin said.

"That's why we had the deadline . . . "

"Yes, that's why we had the deadline. We had to get all three students under wraps before they became contagious, before what they were carrying spread out into the general population."

The end of the weapon was back against his ear. "Contagious from what!" Holman yelled. "Contagious from what!"

Franklin turned to him. "Who cares? No cure, highly contagious. I guess we're in it now, hunh?"

Sinclair said, "Yes, we are."

Holman's eyes were now tearing up. "Screw you both! I didn't volunteer for this, not at all!"

Sinclair said, "Yes, you did. We all volunteered. We all volunteered long ago to serve our country, to follow the orders of our superiors. We've gone places and exposed ourselves to death, day in and day out, in service of this nation. Sometimes this service means going to a foreign country. Sometimes it means staying in-country. And sometimes it means scooping up three college students so they don't infect and possibly kill hundreds of millions of our countrymen, and billions of other people around the world."

Franklin said, "You guys . . . now it makes sense. Nobody would talk to us face to face. We had the aircraft to ourselves in the rear cabins. Me and Holman, we're both orphans. No wives, no family. That's why we were assigned. Wasn't it?"

"That's right," Sinclair said.

Holman's voice was still shaky. "And you, boss. What's your frigging excuse? You an only child, too? You got no family like the two of us?"

"No, I've got brothers and a sister, and both parents still alive."

Franklin said, "And you volunteered? Even when you

knew what was going on?"

"Yes, I did."

Holman said, "Why, for God's sake?"

Sinclair felt the throbbing in his lower back, decided it was now time to take two pain pills instead of just one. "Because, gentlemen, I'm dying of spinal cancer. I'll be dead in a month or two. And I thought that before I went, I could do one more thing for my country. That's why. The men on the wall. That's what I am, and that's what you are, and that's what we do. We defend. Period. Even when the civilians don't know we're even doing it for them. We defend."

For a long while, as the jet sped to the west, there was only the sound of the young girl, coughing and coughing.